THE UNIVERSAL
THEORY
OF IMMIGRATION

THE UNIVERSAL THEORY OF IMMIGRATION

ADAM BETHLEHEM

TRIPLE POINT PRESS

First published in Great Britain in 2016 by
Triple Point Press
2 Hinde Street,
London W1U 2AZ

A CIP catalogue record for this book is available from the British Library.

ISBN: 978-0-9929724-2-4

Designed and typeset by Design 23.
The body of the text is set in Bembo Roman and Bembo Italic.
Bembo was originally designed by Franceso Griffo in the 15th century,
but the modern version was re-cut by Stanley Morison at the Monotype
Corporation in 1929. Printed on Ensocreamy 70.
Printed and bound by Clays Ltd, St Ives plc.

www.triplepointpress.com

For Jennifer

GOD'S PLANE LANDED ON TIME AT HEATHROW AIRPORT. He had thought about Gatwick or Stansted but the idea of the high-speed rail link pleased him. He could have chosen a scheduled flight but he was attentive to his status and determined to travel in style. In any case, precautions had been taken to ensure that his arrival would not be noticed.

The immigration formalities presented no difficulties and, having nothing to declare, he chose the green channel. Everything was going smoothly.

CONTENTS

CONTENTS

THE DECISION

CHAPTER ONE

"Sir, if You'll forgive me, there is a matter that requires... I apologise for the interruption." Gabriel waited for God to speak. This cantankerous mood had been going on for weeks and God's temper had a way of affecting everything. He cleared his throat and waited to see what form their Leader would take this morning. When these cranky states took Him there was no predicting which way things would go.

"All right, get on with it," God was leaning back in his chair and Gabriel was relieved to see He was dressed conservatively. Not that superficial appearances could provide a reliable guide but a beard and flowing robe usually indicated trouble. The thought of another tantrum was terrifying – probably God's intention in the first place. Irritability didn't make for a comfortable life for the rest of them, even if they were in Heaven.

"I'm sure You'll remember the last time someone made an awkward suggestion. Being on the team didn't save Lucifer and we're all terrified of starting something that could be divisive. We haven't quite recovered from that last… ah… situation." Gabriel completed the first part of his speech. It was as far as he had managed to get with his preparations before he had been summoned to the inner sanctum.

"That was gossip. Everyone knows I am forgiving." The atmosphere grew heavy but God had turned his back and was contemplating a view of creation, refusing Gabriel a chance to make his point.

"What I mean, Sir, is that some of us felt there had been a slight over-reaction and it may have been better if… oh dear, I beg Your pardon." Even the apology faded into nothingness as the archangel found himself dismissed from the almighty Presence.

Down below, the world spun slowly on its eccentric axis. Another of the inconsistencies that could have been avoided if He hadn't been so trusting, God thought. If He'd considered these problems for even a single moment, it would have been clear that untested angels weren't ready for responsibility. He should have insisted on close supervision instead of handing over the blueprint and hoping they'd get it right. To be fair, Gabriel hadn't actually been unreliable since his promotion to the top spot. He was a fine figure even after all these years, although recently he had become so… so fussy. It was time for him to take a sabbatical. Any more confused talk would certainly be grounds for dismissal, gross dereliction of duty or something like that. The details could be worked out later.

"We looked at all possibilities, Sir. Without the tilt we had trouble with the seasons. I know You said we shouldn't bother but there were complications and the compromise eradicated many of our problems," Gabriel's hesitant form reappeared in the corner of the office. It wasn't a question of eavesdropping but recently the immortal Being had developed a habit of thinking aloud. "I hope You'll understand if…"

"Didn't I send you away?" God demanded but it was difficult to insist. It wasn't realistic to ask any angel to stay away when he was summoned by a thought.

"We were trying to help." From his position across the table, Gabriel could see his Master had been reading. Today, they were using the mahogany desk from Thailand but it wasn't clear what that meant. Business and tradition? Fairness and reliability? A big change of some sort was coming, that much was evident. God's back was turned and Gabriel leaned in to read the papers on the wooden surface. Contracts? His own… and… Michael?

"Forgive Me, Gabriel. You've done well but I think you should know why you'll be leaving," God was still looking out the window. A decision had been taken.

"You said not to bother You with every detail. That You didn't want to know," Gabriel wasn't sure if his participation was required but what else could he do? If God needed…

"There you go again. You blather on and never get to the point," God turned to face Gabriel. His suit was familiar but rumpled. This had never happened before. Of course they'd all heard rumours but there was no knowing which stories were actually true.

"I'm letting you go," God spoke without emotion. "No no, I don't want to see that mournful look. Your compensation will be adequate and there's no need to be thinking about tribunals."

"Thank you. If You've decided, I shouldn't take up more of Your time. May I ask who'll be replacing me?" Apparently it was going to be Michael. Why else was there a second document on the table? Gabriel was determined to be dignified even if his thoughts were in turmoil. "Would You like me to deal with the handover?"

It was plain to see that God was losing interest. He was muttering under His breath about the perils of favouritism. "Enjoy your holiday," was all He would say.

Michael emerged even as his colleague faded from the scene. He hadn't been in the office since before the Fall and was surpised to discover he was alone. He looked at the figure seated behind the desk. In recent years there had been no reason for a private audience.

"Ah, there you are. I've given Gabriel his marching orders," God broke into the newcomer's thoughts, directed him to the single chair and gestured for him to sit. "Officially We can't say it's permanent and if he's ever fit for duty We may have to take him back. Right then, I'm sure you're anxious to make a start. Remember what happened to your gibbering predecessor and I'm sure you'll settle in."

Gabriel returned. He was accustomed to being summoned back and forth but this time he had thought the ordeal was finally over.

"What are you doing here? I thought We agreed you would take time for reflection." All of a sudden God was on His feet, struggling to contain His temper. For the moment Heaven remained unaltered but on Venus storms were raging.

"Go on, leave, both of you," God dismissed them with a wave. But they were unable to shift; even as He turned His attention elsewhere, they stayed on, like bit-part players in the background.

"Excuse me, Sir," Gabriel was no longer in post but Michael didn't have the experience to deal with a crisis of this magnitude. He resolved to make one last attempt. "There's no easy way of approaching the subject and it makes us look bad going around in circles. Perhaps it would help if You thought we should be more direct?"

"Get on with it! There, you have your instructions. Now spit it out. What the Devil's wrong with you?"

The angels stepped back, ashen where they would once have been radiant. Tales of God's temper may have leaked out in the past but a detail like this had to be kept secret. The D-word could only mean something terrible.

Gabriel looked across at Michael. It was a long time since they had worked together and the junior angel remained as youthful as ever. Maybe God was right. Gabriel could remember a time when he, himself, had been so innocent but the unrelenting pressure had taken its toll. All traces of enthusiasm had disappeared and the need for measured behaviour had created an endless capacity for prevarication and rationalisation. Gabriel shook his head, wondering how much time had passed during these contemplations. Luckily, God had other things on His mind and they were no longer centre stage.

Michael looked across and smiled. It was apparent he didn't understand the peril of their predicament. The Lord of Heaven turned to them with a face of thunder. Michael still had that impish grin. Gabriel braced himself.

"This time you've gone too far." God didn't need to shout, His wrath was all consuming.

The prospect of never-ness and nothing-ness loomed. Before long, no sound would make it over the darkening sea of anger and all would be lost. Wasn't it better to slink away and fail? Slings, arrows, outrageous fortune? The reality hit home but nobody said a word. It was now or never.

Gabriel chose his destiny and stepped forward to ensure Michael was protected. Then, looking directly at their Leader, he spoke with all the courage he could muster:

"It's You who needs the break, Sir! Not me!"

CHAPTER TWO

EVEN AS GABRIEL UTTERED THE WORDS, HE COULD see the face of God changing. An angel may take a decision but freedom of choice was not a realistic option with such an important personage just across the room.

The murky chaos was impenetrable. If God went too far, the separation of light and dark would have to begin all over again. It was possible that next time it wouldn't be Gabriel or Michael trying to keep their feet in a privileged position at the eye of storm. God had hinted recently that He could run things better Himself.

As the designated scapegoat, Gabriel prepared to face his fate but even after a lifetime of signs and wonders he was unprepared. The squall crashed around them, scattering furniture and creating universal confusion. The former archangel held his breath. There had been bad times before. Not everybody would emerge unscathed but when there was only one superpower you had to batten down the hatches and place your trust in fate.

Time itself had been suspended but, gradually, the gloom began to lift. However tenuous, they still had a foothold in Heaven. Gabriel rubbed a weary eye and found one more surprise when he looked around. The tempest had faded along with Michael. The outlook had returned to normal.

Gabriel breathed a sigh of relief although he couldn't help thinking about how erratic life had been recently and that it was naïve to think peace could last. He pulled himself together. It was no use always looking for the black cloud, this was a time to contemplate the silver lining. From the sidelines, he followed as his Leader's thoughts played out across the infinite vastness of His domain. The ominous blackness had receded. The glow that came after was different. Heaven was bright and vivid in every detail.

Before Gabriel's eyes, a troop of apocalyptic horsemen galloped in perfect silence; back and forth, presenting arms, back and forth. Demonstrations of boredom had become commonplace and the angel watched as God's deliberations found expression in rhythmic pattern. The horsemen were swirling around, efficient, threatening, as they paraded in close-knit formation. Then, as if it had been a figment of His imagination,

21

everything was calm. The display had gone, the atmosphere cleared.

"What do you propose?" God asked, looking across at his first lieutenant.

For an instant Gabriel was at a loss. It must have been a long time since he had spoken those rash words.

"I beg Your pardon for speaking so plainly," he braced himself for another tumult but there was no way of avoiding the question.

"You had the right idea, my friend, and I know what's on your mind," God turned away from the window with no hint of temper or impatience. "I'm only asking you to help Me think things through."

Gabriel knew this must be true. How could it have been possible for him to have kept a thought of this importance hidden? He resolved to be bold.

"You've been rather short-tempered recently and I was wondering if You might want a change," he said, hoping the phrasing of his answer as a suggestion would provide a degree of safety.

God sighed but offered no comment.

"Things do run smoothly most of the time..." Gabriel took courage from the atmosphere of disinterested efficiency that indicated a normal working day. "If you like, I could bring Michael in. I'd

22

be happy to distribute responsibility."

He paused but God waved at him to continue.

"I hope that doesn't sound presumptuous, Sir. It's not that we'd take control but we could be caretakers for a short time. I think we'd be able to manage."

Gabriel heard a rhythmical sound. At the edge of his vision, crossing the horizon, a few horsemen walked slowly on parade. Their colours were disturbing. No flying pennants, very drab. God must be deep in thought. More and more horsemen, wheeling and turning in unison.

"Carry on, carry on, I'm still listening," He muttered.

"Why not take a holiday? I'm sure it would be good to get away from all this," Gabriel tried to suppress the feeling of hopefulness. After months of uncertainty, at last they had reached a day of progress. "If something happens I'll make sure nobody loses out while You're away. It would be an example to everyone. For You to rest, I mean. It would show them there's more to Your world than work."

Everything was still and quiet. The entirety of Heaven seemed to be waiting for the Old Man to make a decision.

"Impossible…" God said, once again drifting into

introspection and leaving His right-hand man to wait.

If only Michael were still here, Gabriel thought. At least there'd be someone around to share the burden.

"No, no. Most certainly not!" The machinery of God's vision spluttered into motion. He looked up and gave a start of recognition, almost as though He'd had a nightmare. "Ah, yes. Sorry about that, Gabriel. Fundamental revisions on My mind. There are problems We'll have to deal with sooner or later and I'm not talking about disaster relief or planetary motion."

God had never been interested in detail. He loved the broad brushstrokes and dramatic events but day-to-day management had never been His thing. He'd always told them to keep specifics to themselves.

"You're exceptionally diligent, Gabriel, and I thank you for being attentive. Where were we?"

"I was saying that You might consider a holiday."

"Yes, good idea but I don't think this is the time for Me to leave. Not until these adjustments are under way." God was evidently pleased with Himself, plans formulating which He was disinclined to share.

"My Lord…" the odds were stacked against an underling but Gabriel was determined to make one final effort. "I'm not suggesting the occasional miracle isn't a good idea. It certainly spices things up. But the point is, if You'll forgive me, intervention isn't necessary any more. People are getting on fine without assistance."

"No, I don't see how it could happen. We'll carry on as before but I'll make sure I keep My mind on the job. Thank you, that's all for the moment. We'll meet tomorrow as usual."

"Without meaning to outstay my welcome, I have an idea that might be worth considering." With his heart in his throat, Gabriel crossed the line of propriety. From here-on-forward, there would be no turning back.

"What is it now?" God rumbled. Dark clouds gathered over distant hills but He looked down at His determined deputy and remembered the decision to be less short-tempered.

"How about going to see how things are getting on?" Gabriel suggested. "We get reports from all over but it's not the same as first-hand experience. I should think it would be quite interesting."

God looked down from His window in Heaven. Earth, the subject of a previously completed programme of rectification, drifted into view. Indeed, it was a beautiful place. The other planets were striking in their way but they had a sterile, minimalist, kind

25

of symmetry. The world was certainly special and He was proud to have done the work with so little fuss.

He turned back to the decision waiting to be made. Reluctant as He might be to admit an error, Gabriel had a point. People were designed to help themselves and recently they were throwing up their hands in despair at the least setback. God might try to deny the allegations but He had got into the habit of interfering. Even Heaven had become over-reliant.

What could go wrong if He followed Gabriel's suggestion and left them to their own devices? It would be only for a little while and He could return at short notice if something critical happened.

"Gabriel," He said, speaking as quietly as possible.

"Still here, Sir," came the instantaneous response. The angel knew something was up. The atmosphere had lightened considerably. The anticipation of a holiday had already lifted God's mood.

"I'll be leaving immediately. Clear My diary or arrange things as you think best. Keep a record and I'll deal with your problems *en masse* when I return."

"Of course. Thank you, Sir. Would You like help with the arrangements?"

"No assistance required, thank you very much," God's laughter filled the room. Merriment was almost as disconcerting as the variety of other temperaments on display of late. "I'll be travelling incognito. There's no need for you to worry."

"I..."

"You must learn to relax," God urged his protégé. "You'll be kept busy while I'm away but I know that you've dreamed of being in charge. Do your best and if all goes well We may be in a position to make changes when I come home."

"Thank You, that's very kind," Gabriel faltered, the changes were coming thick and fast. "I'll let You know if something important comes up."

"No, certainly not. I do not want to be contacted. That's the point of the exercise... I'll keep an eye out and you must rest assured I'll come back if I see things are drifting too far."

As He spoke, so it was done.

*

Heaven was a different place without God's overwhelming presence, lighter somehow without the tension of complication and unexpected alteration. Gabriel didn't think God's sabbatical would create too many difficulties. It caused anxiety every time the old chap got involved. You could hardly deny his will but just because he was always right didn't make his prescription the only way to get something done. They needed the break as much as he did.

One last thought. Gabriel hoped his master would be careful. Unusual behaviour of any sort would attract attention. Even a single revelation could turn a discreet holiday into a disturbing fiasco.

VISITOR IN LONDON

CHAPTER THREE

TICKET-MONEY-PASSPORT. TICKET-MONEY-PASSPORT. GOD repeated the mantra that had occupied him since leaving Heaven. The relief when he set off had been tangible and he was looking forward to a proper break from the saintly obsession with detail. In the beginning, every decision had been clear and simple. Plans had been put in place with a minimum of fuss and God had left creation to get on with it. That was then. Now, day-to-day management had assumed undue importance and fact-finding and monitoring had become ends in themselves. *Never mind*, he resolved, if the angels wanted to spend their days wallowing in particulars, good luck to them. It wasn't as if the guiding principles had turned out to be fundamentally wrong. He decided not to think about anything to do with work. Give Gabriel a few days trying to juggle the needs of the dominions and he would be the one needing a rest.

God left the private passenger terminal and followed a succession of moving walkways to mingle with passengers from an incoming commercial flight. He had few plans beyond the essentials and wanted to experience Arrival in all its glory. Earth with its peculiar mixture of beauty and chaos had been the obvious place to get started and God hummed to himself – goodbye drudgery, hello world.

It was splendid, simply wonderful, to be alone for the first time in ages. He strolled along, carrying luggage to complete the disguise and enjoying the unexpected feeling of freedom. Whatever Gabriel had said, there was no doubt in God's mind that he had sufficient resources to overcome the obstacles life might present. On he walked, past the baggage carousels where a large man and his entourage were at the centre of attention. Photographs were being taken while, in the background, suitcases meandered mournfully along a conveyor belt.

God's mind was drifting as he entered the green channel with a throng of travellers. A journey could be too busy if everything were planned and he had no intention of wasting the opportunity before him. He would behave like a local and try to blend in. That was the way to discover a city, or so he had heard. It would certainly be interesting.

He wondered where to go first. The train into town,

of course, and then he would find accommodation. Why exactly had he chosen London? It wasn't the oldest of the great cities, nor the most beautiful. Gabriel probably would have expected him to go to Jerusalem or even Rome. Then he remembered... it must have happened last week when old angel Blake had popped in for a chat. People might have been created equal but sometimes, very occasionally, a personality materialised on the scene who was simply special. Spontaneous, that was the thing about William, and a unique way of looking at the world. There was something he had said – God could barely remember the words – something about modernity versus the stultifying weight of history. In any case, it was doubtful anyone had overheard their discussion so he was well and truly free. No miracles, no fuss. This time he could experience the world instead of observing from a distance.

What kind of hotel should he choose? Somewhere intimate and friendly with a café nearby for breakfast and small talk about the weather. Then he would see the museums and galleries or whatever it was that kept visitors entertained.

"Good morning, sir. If I can ask you to bear with me for a few minutes of your time."

The tall figure that was God stopped and looked around. Gabriel must have found out where he was going and sent the young man in his uniform to make sure everything was going well. Angels, as a group, were inclined to fuss but Gabriel should have known better. They had agreed he would have time on his own. A city was hardly dangerous and he had managed more difficult tasks before. Never mind, there was no need to be impolite, the boy was only doing his duty.

"*Good morrow, young sire,*

Pray tell your desire," God offered.

The customs officer looked carefully at the man of indeterminate age standing before him in what seemed to be theatrical robes. Aside from the gentleman's clothing and accent, there was something unusual he couldn't quite put a finger on. The Arrivals team had been briefed about the billionaire travelling *incognito* but they had been told to expect an oriental prince, not some olde-worldy English gent. He took the decision to be extra vigilant. Appearances could be deceptive. All sorts of weird and wonderful creatures were arriving in London these days.

"Would you show me your luggage?" he put out a hand to stop the new arrival.

God wasn't sure what was required. His interlocutor

was overweight and clearly needed to spend time on personal presentation.

"Do...You...Understand?" the dishevelled official continued with a confidence incompatible with the inferiority of his social position.

The young man was concentrating on speaking slowly but even he noticed the darkening of the atmosphere. In Heaven, Gabriel had complained about the effect of God's moods on his surroundings; on Earth, there was a different explanation.

"Never mind about the lights. We've had trouble with our electricity supplies recently. I'll have a quick look in the bags. Please don't worry, the government has prescribed targets for random inspections. This process is entirely routine." Not quite true but something needed to be said because the eccentric traveller had become unduly disturbed.

God recovered his composure. The well-mannered words provided welcome relief and it became clear the confrontation had nothing to do with Gabriel. The disguise had worked. The customs officer showed no sign of having recognised the visitor and was going about his business as usual. Immediately the feeling of gloom lifted and God placed both his briefcase and the larger bag on the bench for inspection.

"And there you are, sir, the lights are back on. These power cuts play havoc with our computers."

Once again God was surprised by the weight given to purely practical explanations. Had they no interest in the dominance and influence of Heaven? Nevertheless, he chose not to comment and allowed the examination to continue.

"No need for us to worry about all that. I'll have a quick look and then you can be on your way. On holiday, are you?"

"*A fortnight's rest from years of toil,*

A brief respite from years of work," God said, doing his best to make a good impression.

How strange, the officer thought, and why was he wearing a cape? Not only old-fashioned but also inappropriate in the heat. Still, such things were hardly relevant and there was no crime in outlandish dress. The gentleman was no stranger than the succession of musicians who passed through every week. With a mental reminder about the need to keep an open mind, he moved on without a rush to judgement. He popped open the catches on the suitcase and flipped back the lid – to find that the case was entirely empty.

The young man took a step backwards and considered the increasingly curious state of affairs.

35

His colleagues might be setting him up. They were probably gathered round the CCTV having a good laugh. Well, he would give them no joy. Behave with complete professionalism. That would be the way to handle this one.

"Can you explain please?" he looked at God, not aggressive but assertive. As he spoke, he reached for the briefcase which, to his relief, contained a toothbrush and a few personal items of clothing.

"Explain?" God shifted uncomfortably while he tried to understand what was required. There was no change in the lighting which he took to be an indication of self-control. "Ah, yes. I have brought luggage so that I may take souvenirs when I return. My assistant encouraged me to make the adventure. I will make purchases when I have arranged passage and an abode near the centre. It is not Sunday and merchants will be available for trade."

God waited to see if these plans, vague as they might be, would satisfy the self-confident figure of authority.

On the other side of the table the customs man noticed that the newcomer's manner of speech had changed. This must mean the traveller was an actor sent by colleagues to fool him. Then again, it could be an assessment. He should be extra careful.

"In that case I suggest you tell me where you bought the bags. They are unusual both in material and in the style of their construction."

"Of course," God smiled, delighted to have a comprehensible query at long last. "I created them myself so as not to attract attention." He wondered whether it was appropriate to give further background to his journey but concluded the information could only be confusing.

The man looked at his subject with increasing scepticism. Stranger and stranger. If it were a joke, it wasn't funny. And if not... well, there was something distinctly inconsistent about this person whose voice and accent kept changing. He informed the gentleman that he would need to wait while the cases were inspected and invited him to take a seat in a side room.

In the isolation of the secure cubicle, God contemplated his position. It was an elementary blunder. The Elizabethan Age had been an enticing prospect, so easy and... it was Blake's fault, with his tales of English grandeur, world trade and the intellectual life. He drew a deep breath. To have been caught by such an error on his first day could have been embarrassing. But then, nobody knew he was in

London so the mistake would go unnoticed.

An adjustment was easily accomplished and God disposed of the offending clothing. He knew he should have listened to Gabriel's advice about the nuances of life but if he had stopped to consider every admonition and recommendation, there would have been no point in making the trip. He could easily have stayed in Heaven.

The junior officer returned with the two items that had been prodded and probed and definitively X-rayed. There were no hidden compartments and God couldn't be detained any longer. It turned out not to be a joke after all. Behind the scenes, the full complement of the customs community had been gathered before the bank of television monitors to watch the arrival of the eastern gentleman who was rumoured to be the most influential person ever to arrive at Heathrow. Nobody knew the potentate's real name but you could tell he was special simply by the size of him.

This time the youngster was accompanied by a colleague who had offered to take a look at the eccentric holidaymaker but, when they returned to the little room, there was nothing unusual or suspicious about God who was sitting quietly on a plastic chair.

He was wearing an old-fashioned but acceptable suit, the cap and feather had disappeared into a pocket and the cape was buried in the dustbin. All in all, the traveller looked reasonably normal and he couldn't be detained for carrying an empty suitcase. The bags were duly returned and God was invited to leave.

As he was exiting through the sliding doors, the senior man turned to his colleague with a grin. The young fellow had a distinctly queasy look, probably needed a lie down after another heavy night. These lads, burning the candle at both ends. Well, they would learn, time enough to be wise when they got older.

★

God was relieved he had managed to escape undetected. He had never travelled before and there was a lot to take in. Bolstered by good intentions, he took up his cases and walked through the door leading to the Arrivals hall. The technicalities of border control were complete and he was looking forward to experiencing London with its multitude of earthly pleasures.

CHAPTER FOUR

GOD LEFT THE HEATHROW EXPRESS WITH A SPRING in his step. He could manage his cases without difficulty and the pinstripe looked perfect, both smart and comfortable, giving him confidence for the adventure that lay ahead.

Around him, Paddington Station was a varied cacophony of sound. Announcements could be heard echoing overhead and regular travellers walked briskly along the platform, each pursuing an individual objective without direction from any visible authority. His education had started, God realised, and Gabriel would have been pleased to see the progress already made. He brought his mind back to the matter at hand. Near the ticket office there was a kiosk advertising 'Tourist Information'. He strolled, unhurried, ready for the answer to all his questions.

Two young women in the brightly coloured booth were engaged in dispensing advice. A satisfied customer walked away leaving one free and God made his way to the counter putting on his most agreeable face. He remembered his earlier *faux pas* and knew he needed to speak modern British. There was a great deal of muttering from behind his back but the young lady spoke kindly and without any trace of impatience.

"Sorry, dear, there's a bit of a queue today. You'll have to wait like everybody else."

God blushed and stammered out his apologies. It was going to take a while to understand the subtleties of life. Still, it was early in the day and he was willing to learn. He took his place as the line moved slowly forward.

All those details he had avoided so assiduously in Heaven were evidently important. A thought about Gabriel crossed his mind briefly but the miscellany on display was too distracting. How bland Heaven was by comparison. It was obviously different in London but then, standing in a queue for tourist information, one was bound to see strange people. Most surprising was a degree of informality he could never have anticipated. A girl in the queue ahead turned to look at him. Had he been thinking aloud?

She was surrounded by a group of friends and God could hear them speaking Italian, commenting on his accent as they moved to the front of the line. The tourist information officer spoke only English and they were laughing while they tried to communicate. Clearly it was amusing. God couldn't help feeling sensitive but they could have been talking about anything at all.

When his turn came, he strode smartly to the counter determined to put the latest misfortune firmly in the past. He addressed the young woman formally, asking for advice about hotels and the best way to the centre of town. Thanks to his business-like demeanour and command of the situation, the information was provided without delay.

To one side, the gibbering group of young tourists were floundering in their macaronic English. He could have helped but this time they would have to struggle. Not that they'd remember. People had a remarkable capacity for forgetting, particularly if it were to their advantage. He gathered up a map and a collection of pamphlets then, thanking the advisor, he turned and set off to find a taxi.

A fleet of cabs waited. They all looked the same so God chose the car at the front of the row thereby proving that fairness and justice were alive on Earth as they should be in Heaven. Langham Place near Regent Street was his first port of call and he restrained surprise at the realisation that his driver was to be a woman. He asked if she had heard of the hotel recommended by the tourist advisor.

"Of course, grand big place it is too. Built in the heritage style. Jump in."

God smiled and thought it sounded perfect. He would get a feeling for England immediately. The driver was chatting away. It must be a lonely job sitting behind the plastic screen travelling up and down for hours. No wonder she wanted to talk.

"Personally, I can't see the point of coming to London and staying somewhere that's like every other place on Earth. It's fine for a businessman like yourself..." she relaxed into the conversation. "You want to be in a convenient place with all the mod cons but tourists get the wrong impression. They follow other travellers around for a few weeks, eat in places they recognise from home and then back they go to tell their friends how quaint we are. What's the point of coming at all?"

It was unmistakeably a favourite topic. All God could see of his driver was a pair of blue eyes reflected in the rear-view mirror.

"What they want to do is stay at home and watch

the telly but I suppose that would be no good for us. Good for the traffic and the ozone layer... cab trade would probably suffer."

God looked out the window as the streets drifted by. He knew she was right. He should have stuck to his original plan about finding a quiet hotel but he was following the recommendation from the kiosk at Paddington Station. He needed to rest, and it wasn't only the stress of negotiating the airport and the complications of a railway system. The grand hotel would have to do until he had got his strength back. Things would look better after a good night's sleep. He was sure of it.

The taxi pulled into the slip road at the top of Langham Place and stopped before the hotel's doorman. She was still talking but paused to offer a receipt.

"I do go on a bit. I'm sorry, I'm having quite a day, what with my father being ill and my children..." She glanced at the banknotes and smiled. "Do you have anything smaller?"

The money didn't matter to God. She could keep the change. He blessed her and wished her happiness, giving assurances that the father would feel better too. That should help cheer her up.

She thanked him and handed over a business card.

If he wanted a driver for the day, she could show him the parts of London a tourist couldn't usually reach. Then, after another smile, she turned back into the bustle of life in the capital, wished him luck and drove off.

★

God watched as the cab entered the stream of traffic and was swallowed up. All of a sudden, Heaven felt far away. He was pleased with his blessing though. After the trials and tribulations of the day, it had allowed him to feel almost normal. He glanced down at the card in his hand – a telephone number and the taxi company's name – and wondered if he would see her again. As a matter of practicality, he could think about contacting her for the authentic tour as she had suggested.

Inside the hotel, procedures at the reception desk were reminiscent of the gates of Heaven but the questions were formulaic and mostly about payment and the length of stay. It was only a few minutes before a suite had been arranged and the empty suitcase whisked away by an enthusiastic porter. The hotel cultivated an air of efficiency but God hung on to the briefcase with his passport and money and declined a wake-up call because he was feeling exhausted. Something to do with travel he thought as he followed directions to the lift. Nothing similar had happened in the past but he should learn not to be surprised. It was a holiday and there were bound to be new experiences on an expedition this far away from Heaven.

CHAPTER FIVE

THE CURTAINS HAD BEEN LEFT PARTLY OPEN AND A haze of light filled the hotel bedroom. God slept on, enjoying a dream as fulfilling as any thought he'd had in Heaven. On through an earthly paradise he drifted, across rolling fields and sun-drenched meadows until he touched down in a building filled with chintzy furnishings. The style was unfamiliar but imagination accepts no limitation and the vision was sufficiently detailed to seem real.

Time passed, waves of sleep buffeting gently until he stirred and the disorientation of wakefulness slowly cleared. The bedroom, unlike his dream, was bland with pastel colours and unremarkable marble fittings. The rumble of traffic was barely distracting and there was no particular reason to move except for the unnerving feeling of loneliness. Usually by this time a deputation would have appeared asking for advice or needing to discuss solutions to some intractable problem. He hadn't imagined the solitary life being so depressing. It might be an idea to go to the dining room where there would be other visitors and perhaps even the chance to chat.

After a quick shower, he wandered downstairs through the lobby to ask directions for somewhere to eat. It was already late morning but, the receptionist assured him, there was no reason to worry about the time. God was welcome to make use of the bistro, the formal dining room or the lobby café. And, of course, room service would be available twenty-four hours a day.

The main restaurant, on the top floor, was busy but a member of staff directed him to a table near the picture windows overlooking Portland Place. God took his seat among a pleasing crowd of guests, very few of whom were dressed formally. It was a thought that provided a subtle reminder of things to be done before his holiday could get properly underway. To have arrived without a change of clothing had been hopelessly unrealistic but he could go shopping like the normal man he was determined to be. He dismissed the matter along with residual thoughts of retribution after the discomfort at the airport. It was time to move on. This was a new day and, if there were lessons to be learnt, he could start immediately.

Once he was settled, a waiter approached and

offered a menu. Taking the opportunity for personal contact, God asked the young man for advice. He explained that he was new in town and had arrived on the previous day – what he really wanted was an English breakfast. The waiter was undaunted by the request and needed only to note the guest's room number. Tea or coffee? God was in two minds but chose tea, thinking it would be more appropriate. Mostly he was pleased that his first attempt at conversation had not been taken amiss.

Around him sightseers were consulting schedules and timetables, planning the day's activities in a systematic fashion. He couldn't help overhearing the arrangements of the middle-aged couple sitting nearby. Theatres, museums, exhibitions. When these two went back home having tramped every street, they would enjoy their memories more than the holiday itself. In addition, they would have a video recording as a reminder in case their attention took a break during the heavy day. As God looked on, the energetic pair hefted their backpacks and photographic equipment and set out on their first mission.

The dining room was emptying and God glanced through a selection of newspapers while he waited for his food. The big political stories, retold in various forms in different publications, were reasonably familiar. For millennia people had been asking for intervention on one side or the other. Both the scandals and the personalities had a tendency to recur although the names did change from generation to generation. Letters to the Editor, worthy and well-intentioned as usual; and finally columns and columns of personal advertisements that were altogether more interesting than the fantasy world of sport.

God wondered how he would describe himself if he had to place a notice. He could simply write *God*. That, of course, covered everything although it would do little to make himself sound appealing. And to refer to past successes might be dangerously pompous. Plans are more important than achievements but then his major project was underway and he couldn't confess to an ambition to carry on as before. Everybody needs something new to aim for. His work may be important but he felt stale. Looking for new projects? Looking for new pastures? That wouldn't look good in print.

He was rescued from further consideration by the young gentleman bearing a platter with his breakfast. Eggs, sausages, tomatoes and beans. Almost everything was recognisable except for the aroma of smoked bacon that was an assault on senses protected for many years. A simple taste was sufficient to confirm an unsettling suspicion and the deduction was easily made – nothing so tasty could be bad and the injunction against porcine products would have to be placed under review. It would be a minor project and certainly something that could wait until he returned to Heaven. After years of abstinence there was sure to be dissent but Gabriel could be relied on to bring the community into line. Change was no bad thing. After a few ritual objections, the society of Heaven would be celebrating the enticing prospect of progress.

The waiter wasn't busy, God could ask for more advice.

"Of course. How can I help?" the young man said, tucking a tray under one arm as he waited, ready to fulfil his duty.

"As you know, this is my first time in London. I... ah... I hope you can understand my English," God spoke hesitantly.

"No problem, sir. You speak fluently and your accent is very good."

"I have had opportunities to practise. There are many Englishmen where I live. I am a great admirer of your country." He didn't explain Blake's error and the waiter politely forbore from asking personal details.

"Now that I'm here," God continued with growing confidence. "I would like to make sure I experience the reality of this wonderful city. I don't want to leave having seen only museums and the tourist routes. What would you advise me to do?"

"I know what you mean about museums. Do you have any particular interests?" The waiter considered the matter seriously.

Now, that was a question. God could easily say he was fascinated by everything and that not a single detail would escape his attention. Unfortunately, he had discovered there were gaps in his knowledge and that was no longer true.

"I'm interested in most subjects. On the other hand, I don't have to work today so I'd like to do something a Londoner might do to relax." God was still tired despite the long rest and a few hours of recreation would be a reasonable way to start the holiday.

"It's difficult for me to tell you. I'm not from the city myself although I've been here a few years. Let me think."

God checked to see whether his breakfast was getting cold. It would be disrespectful to continue eating while they spoke.

"If I didn't have to work? In this weather, I think I'd be outdoors… You could go to Regent's Park," a wistful air had overtaken the waiter's face as he imagined a day in the sunshine. "It's not far and there's a good view over the city from Primrose Hill. I suppose if you had children, you'd take them to the zoo. Have you noticed, sir, how people of all ages love doing children's activities?"

The visiting deity was surprised and grateful for the recommendation. He had more questions but the polite young man excused himself to attend to a new party of diners. Always in search of information, God looked around. Nobody was watching and he took out the guidebook he had kept hidden in a pocket to disguise his tourist status. He made short work of breakfast and took a second cup of tea, relaxing as he read about the magic of Primrose Hill.

CHAPTER SIX

THE SUNSHINE WAS GLORIOUS AS GOD WALKED OUTSIDE and stood under the hotel's portico looking along the full length of Portland Place. To the north, in the middle distance, trees and greenery showed the way to Regent's Park. It was warmer than he had expected with a few wispy clouds and the trace of a breeze to take the edge off the heat of the day. *Unseasonal weather*, the receptionist had said when she saw him setting off but to God who was used to the steady cool of Heaven, the change was something of a treat. He walked briskly. The pavements were broad and clear even if the roadway were filled with cars waiting impatiently for a change of signals. How beautiful this must have been before traffic was invented, if indeed anybody ever noticed the quiet and elegance of a well-planned street.

At Marylebone Road he followed other pedestrians towards the crossing and an inkling of the effort behind the scenes emerged before his eyes. The world had become very organised, **LOOK RIGHT – LOOK LEFT** written in the roadway. It had been easy to dismiss Gabriel's obsession with detail but conceivably there was value to the team's work. Although they appeared to have forgotten that anybody who could read instructions in English would be used to cars. What about visitors from other countries who couldn't read the language? Had anybody thought about them?

God considered the position as he waited at the traffic lights. He was unaware that a sub-committee of the Department of the Environment had been convened to consider the very point, one more fact among many unobserved from the lofty heights of Heaven. The value of writing on the roadway had been demonstrated and it had not been necessary to separate locals from other newcomers. A pedestrian is on foot whatever his or her social background and there was no reason to think that tourists were at a disadvantage.

"Hmph," was all God could think as the little green man beckoned and he set off to cross the road.

A short distance past a terrace of private houses and God found himself at the entrance to the park. After a morning of adventure, he might have been prepared but the riot of colour and perfume left him standing, open-mouthed, speechless at the splendour of this corner of London, a city chosen from many in the infinity of creation. Where to begin? He followed the central avenue between cherry trees surrounded by a carpet of the greenest grass. So very, incredibly, beautiful. And everybody was smiling. Could an abundance of joyfulness have something to do with the weather? If sunshine were good for the world, what was the purpose of clouds or storms or even winter? God thought awhile, sure that he should have answers to fundamental questions at his fingertips. If only he had listened to Gabriel and paid more attention.

Surely it must be superfluous for each tree to be covered with such a profusion of coloured blossoms? But then, so many things that made the world better felt unnecessary. Did flowers have a purpose? Or tasty food, or beauty in general? God caught himself looking at the young people basking in the sunshine – more fashions like the travellers at the train station and yet none of them seemed to be worried about being conspicuous.

He turned away from distraction and concentrated on the oversized notice board with a map. The route was simple enough. He would walk up through the formal gardens and then past the zoo. God liked animals but, as the waiter had said, he was travelling without children and had no excuse to enjoy himself. Leaving behind all temptation, he set off slowly past the fountains.

It was surprising to see how many people were out and about during the week. Some should have been at work but had given in to temptation. He found himself smiling as he walked and a small note of triumph entered his thoughts. Here was the reason for variations in the climate – nothing would get done in unrelenting good weather. The realisation was comforting but the contentment wouldn't last. God had never had time for frivolity and was inclined to be irritable unless he was actively engaged. The day's task was Primrose Hill. After that he could think about matters of practicality.

He pressed on across open fields, reminding himself that he was here to explore the world, not only look at it. There were others on the grass playing silly games and chasing dogs. He stopped briefly to watch. Here was something else without particular purpose. Not precisely true, he couldn't help noting. Dogs have a purpose but games are usually designed to be pointless. The people didn't look competitive as they hurled and chased a plastic disc, yet each one gave an impression of happiness.

The problem was vaguely unsettling and God was deep in thought, barely noticing his surroundings as he passed the zoo and progressed up the gentle slope of Primrose Hill. The city was laid out in panorama and looking out from the viewing platform God put aside his worries and decided to experience the world as it appeared before his eyes. Some landmarks were familiar. The river was hidden from view but he spotted Paul's church easily. Even at a distance it was striking and impressive although it was dwarfed in size by more modern constructions.

He looked for somewhere to sit. All the nearby benches were occupied but other visitors were resting in the uncut grass on the slope of the hill. Why not? The park was perfectly safe and no one would recognise or even notice him. He chose a quiet area away from the paved pathways and cast off his inhibitions. After a brief glance around, he rolled his jacket into a ball for a pillow and, within seconds, he was asleep.

CHAPTER SEVEN

IT WAS NEARLY LUNCHTIME WHEN GOD AWOKE TO FIND himself surrounded by picnicking families. A single swallow danced high above and clouds drifted past, soft and very close. Young children played busily, each watched over by a hovering, attentive parent. God knew people would always be fruitful. They would no more be able to forgo procreation than they could resist hunger, pain or the need to feel important. That part of the programme, at least, was proceeding according to plan.

He sat up and stretched. The sun was strong and he would need protection if this was going to be a regular event. Had he remembered? There was a brief flurry of anxiety as he checked the pockets of his jacket but the wallet and his money were safe. There was no chance of forgetting the guidebook. The next time he could leave it at the hotel.

He found his way down the hill to a village filled with restaurants and coffee bars, ambling past window displays and enjoying the liberty of independence.

Busiest of all was a public house at the end of the road where a group of people had gathered around rough wooden benches. The rumbling of his stomach, an earthly sign of human need, was a reminder of the attention that must be paid to practical matters. In Heaven these things might take care of themselves but this world demanded sleep, food and drink, and probably a host of other complications yet to be considered.

There was a sign on the terrace written in a pretence of old English – patrons were advised to order food and drink at the bar. The directions were clear and simple.

God found a seat at a newly vacated table and edged into the shade of an umbrella. A tall beaker of beer stood untouched on the table before him and he watched beads of moisture gathering, sliding slowly down the glass onto the wooden surface. The guidebook lay unopened as he took a first tentative sip. The pale yellow liquid had an unexpectedly bitter taste, not unpleasant but... *cold*, was the first impression. He drank again, enjoying the feeling of refreshment as the draught slipped down. Soon he was finding his way to the bar for another pint and it wasn't long before he was back in the sunshine.

Without appearing too interested, he watched a group of drinkers on the forecourt of the pub. They were wearing dust-covered working clothes and most had plastic hats although some were drinking bareheaded. They were trying to attract women but their efforts were crude, even vulgar. They would probably have more success if they smartened up and behaved. Then again, he paused to drink, what did he know about the rules of these relationships?

Never before had he bothered with the intricacies of companionship and it was obvious that Heaven would be a more attractive proposition if he had a confidante to return home to. What would she be like? Beautiful, of course, and kind. She would accept that his work was important but she would have her own career and wouldn't be overawed by his achievements. When he thought about it, Heaven had become exceedingly tedious. Unrelenting work, work, work. Always people wanting things, demanding action and intervention. A deep breath, almost like a sob, bubbled to the surface. Luckily nobody had noticed. The few remaining workmen were focused on a group of schoolgirls who were enjoying the attention. The remainder of the terrace was empty. Lunch hour had ended and people were drifting back to work.

God pulled himself together. Long ago he had chosen this path and he would have to live with the consequences. There was little point in cultivating feelings of regret and there was certainly nobody else to take responsibility. He stood up, feeling off-balance and dizzy. It hadn't taken long to walk to the park and he could be back at the hotel very soon.

He turned as he set off, almost knocking over the collection of empty glasses on his table although he couldn't recall having ordered more than two. None of this mattered at all. He had been drinking for more than an hour and his thoughts might be clouded but one thing had become abundantly clear – he'd had enough of holiday. It was time to be going home.

CHAPTER EIGHT

GOD TOOK A FEW STEPS FROM THE PUB AND FOUND himself standing on a short bridge over a railway line. The route was unfamiliar and he struggled to concentrate as the slope meandered downhill. No matter that he called out for assistance, neither angel nor lowly citizen appeared to lend a hand.

"Shame on you," said a woman with blue hair as he lurched into a lamppost, holding on until he managed to regain equilibrium.

Nobody else gave a second glance. In other parts of London, a rumpled old gentleman may have attracted attention but God had stumbled from leafy Primrose Hill into Camden Town which was used to all kinds of life. He clung on and considered his options. He wanted home or at least to find the hotel but all of a sudden he was hungry. There was no sensible way of making a choice so he picked the closest restaurant where a cartoon picture of a cheerful chicken stood proudly above the doorway. Through the window he could see uniformed cooks in a gleaming kitchen with fans turning on the ceiling above the dining area. The sight of platters overflowing with chicken, salad and chips made the decision easy.

Leaving the safety of the lamppost, he crossed the pavement and reached the big glass door. Incredibly, no matter how hard he pushed, it refused to open. There were other places to eat but each rejection felt like failure. God was too upset to realise how easy life could have been if he had taken the trouble to read the PULL sign painted on the doorway. It would have been almost as easy as crossing the road.

He was considering his next move when the door opened in his face and he was forced to stand back to allow a well-fed group onto the sidewalk. Without further consideration, he put his foot in the doorway and walked in before anyone could object.

"Good afternoon, sir, can I help you?" a smiling assistant waited behind the counter, ready to take God's order.

If only I could tell you, he thought, but reminded himself to concentrate on lunch. He looked at the menu for inspiration.

"A meal for one?" he suggested hopefully.

The food didn't take long to arrive and God's situation

looked brighter as time passed. In Heaven he had thought solely in terms of kill or cure, dark or light, and it hadn't been obvious that drink would have only a temporary effect. Sitting in a booth near the back of the restaurant, the subtle gradations of ordinary life provided comfort and he felt better as he worked his way through a bowlful of salty fries before starting on a second serving of chicken. Every experience must have intrinsic value and to understand loneliness was surely as valuable a lesson as any he could hope to learn.

The meal had been delicious and it was time to face the world again. He found the washroom and stood before the mirror, combing wisps of grass from his hair and brushing down his jacket. This time he negotiated the door without difficulty and found himself standing at the side of Chalk Farm Road. The route to the park was some way off but a taxi materialised and he was spared the indignity of having to wait on the pavement.

The driver, rough-looking with tattoos and a single golden earing, could be heard speaking but this time the journey felt different. The man had a small telephone attached to his ear and flagrantly ignored his customer as they crawled through the traffic. *It would have been quicker to walk*, God muttered, feeling disgruntled at being side-lined. Unfortunately, he was lost after a few twists and turns in the back ways of Camden and had no choice but to stay in the taxi; certainly the lesser of the two evils.

The driver was oblivious to his passenger's mounting irritation. The call ended and he shouted back without having the courtesy to turn around, "Sorry, guv, traffic's awful. Speed bumps, cycle lanes, any excuse for digging up the roads."

"So I see." It was God's turn to be cool. He wasn't going to chat to fill this mindless motorist's schedule. He had plenty of change so there was no chance of handing out large notes.

The man was already back on his telephone. The cab pulled away from the traffic lights, turned the corner and... God recognised Regent's Park. The familiar surroundings bolstered his confidence and he called to the driver to stop. He wasn't sure what to expect, protest or possibly an argument, but again he had misjudged the situation. The cabbie pulled over and took the fare with no complaint. He even broke into his new call to wish the old fellow a pleasant evening before lighting up and speeding off.

God was alone again but at least he was by himself. The gardens were just as beautiful as he recalled and despite the fading sunshine there were still people enjoying the day as shadows lengthened across the green. The terraced buildings were looking particularly elegant. If he had lived in London, he would have chosen a house looking directly on to the park.

As before, Marylebone Road was filled with traffic and Portland Place was the same picture of elegance God remembered from the start of his dramatic day. A group of worshippers had gathered near the Chinese embassy and policemen were on duty guarding the entrance although the situation had an air of remarkable calm. The eastern sects were certainly powerful. They must command enormous respect for people to be praying in the street.

He stopped on Portland Place where the road curved down towards Regent Street. His recall of the little difficulty after the pub was fading along with the resolve to remember the feelings of loneliness and despair. With the power of rationalisation that had sustained him in difficult times before this journey, God noted that forgetfulness can be a valuable tool in negotiating the challenges of life. Since people were created in his image, he could no more escape the similarities than could they. Already, his mind was turning to the night ahead.

THE UNIVERSAL THEORY OF IMMIGRATION

He looked at the building standing gracefully opposite his hotel. A church for All Souls. It was a beautiful idea, inclusive and worthy, and something that could be considered when he had time. A bath, a drink and he'd be ready to see the sights.

CHAPTER NINE

IT WAS EVENING OF THE SECOND DAY, GOD REMINDED himself, which meant it was still Thursday. He had been so busy running up and down Primrose Hill that he hadn't managed to get to the shops for the extra clothes he had planned to buy. That would be a task for the morning and he was looking forward to the evening's activities with an unfamiliar mixture of anxiety and anticipation.

Across the road from the hotel, not far from the entrance to All Souls, was a building bearing the legend *BBC*. A long queue had formed. A performance of some sort, he guessed, noticing that people were clutching brightly coloured tickets and chatting in enthusiastic little groups. He had money but was looking forward to something a little more exciting than a seat in a darkened theatre. A holiday demanded activity rather than the passive exercise of sitting and watching. Besides, it could be lonely as a singleton in a room full of strangers. Proximity didn't bring company although it might be different for these people who had always lived on top of each other.

He crossed the road and walked pensively along the pavement. He was used to space and comfort and it had been distinctly uncomfortable sitting with complete strangers on the train from the airport. Most English people evidently felt as he did although their children behaved differently, and it was the same with visitors from other countries. Possibly garrulousness and gaiety had something to do with a holiday.

Hyper-intellectualisation was a transparent defence against loneliness and God knew exactly what was happening. Show him a problem, any kind of pressure, and he would end up giving a lecture even if there were no-one around to listen. Gabriel and Peter had never said anything but it was always obvious what they thought. Why bother to deny the truth? He was always going on about something he had done, pretending it was interesting. Obviously it was a trap to depend on past glories instead of believing that better was yet to come. The cult of scepticism was growing and they called it science but it was only an attempt to replace him. Who exactly did those cynics think had created logic? It didn't matter, the world wasn't simple any more and he could move with the times. Nobody could accuse him of standing still, even less of being unambitious.

"*Onward and upward,*" he said.

"Hello?" a lady was addressing him from her position in the queue.

He hadn't realised he was thinking aloud. Not that it mattered, these ideas weren't particularly secret. God looked at the woman trying to determine whether it was appropriate to reply. After a brief moment he recognised her – it was the taxi driver who had brought him to the hotel.

She was alone in the queue. In front, a couple were engaged in an intimate embrace and behind there was a larger group. He was careful not to look as if he were insinuating himself for fear of starting an argument. She was asking about his holiday, was he enjoying his time in London?

"Indeed, indeed. Perhaps I spent too long in the sunshine," God said, feeling the need to explain his colour. He didn't want her to think he was blushing. "How about you? Were you at work today?"

She didn't notice his lack of experience with casual conversation or, if she did, she politely ignored his difficulties. She had a lovely smile and looked altogether happier now that she wasn't driving. The blue of her jacket almost matched the colour of her eyes.

71

"Not today. I share the cab with my partner and it was his turn."

God knew this word. He was in favour of marriage and the informality implied by a partnership was demeaning. People should be more serious about their relationships, he thought, but he was aware that on holiday opinions like these were best kept to himself.

"Well, it's been a beautiful day and I wasn't expecting the weather. Let's hope it will continue for a few more days," he pressed on, unsure if the subject were appropriate. "I hope you enjoy your play."

"It's not a play," she told him. "It's a radio programme, the News Quiz. I always listen when I'm driving and I was invited tonight by Ben. I hope he's not late..."

As she spoke a handsome young man arrived, tall and dark haired, and stood beside her in the queue. Her face lit up and God took his leave to avoid embarrassment. He set off towards Regent Street with a trace of regret and feeling more than a little preoccupied. *Much younger than her*, he was thinking. Not that it mattered. He'd assumed her partner would be nearer her own age, that was all.

*

"Who's your admirer, Mum?" the young man gave a cheesy grin.

"Oh, stop it. He's someone I had in the cab yesterday. Very nice. A bit anxious but a good man underneath it all, I would say. A little shy."

"Sorry I chased him away. I should have waited while you got to know him better. Does he have a name?"

She was distracted by a hidden thought and didn't hear the question. It wasn't often she met someone she could talk to. She'd been so despondent lately and conversation with the passengers wasn't usually her thing. To find herself jabbering away had been a shock. And then seeing him again this evening? Well, perhaps it wasn't such a coincidence, after all she had dropped him at the hotel across the road. He had an unusual accent and his clothes were a trifle strange.

Ben was smiling at her, properly this time.

"What's wrong?" she asked.

"Nothing." He looked at his mother thoughtfully.

"Good," she said bravely. "Now tell me, how have you been?"

"Mum, come on. Stop trying to pretend. Forget the Quiz, you can catch up with him if you go now." He could still see the gentleman, not far off, walking down towards the church.

"Don't be silly," not that she wasn't tempted. Her passenger was good-looking and carried his years easily, couldn't be much older than... She forced herself to turn away. Women of her age didn't chase men in the street, especially not if they were strangers. Just like Ben to push things too far. "I'm with you tonight," she said.

Neither spoke again but he put an arm around her shoulders. Luckily the queue began to move and they were soon inside. If it were meant to be, it would have been, she thought. Sometimes you had to seize the opportunity but now he had gone and that was that. In a few days, he would be only a little regret and then, eventually, she would forget about him altogether.

CHAPTER TEN

GOD WATCHED FROM THE STEPS OF THE CHURCH AS the queue filtered towards the entrance. She was the first person he had met in London and if her partner hadn't arrived he would probably have wanted to see her again. It was a stroke of luck to have discovered the truth before anything distressing had occurred.

The line of ticket holders was filtering slowly into the building. *Like a trail of insects*, he thought, but the truth was that if he had been offered the chance he would have been delighted to be one of those little people participating in something greater than themselves. As always, he was on the outside looking in. God turned back to the church. It should have been comforting in his hour of need but the doors were closed and two bearded men were arranging sleeping bags in the corner of the covered walkway. He didn't want to think about anything so disheartening. He was already shaken by unfamiliar feelings and a comparison with his own sleeping arrangements could only lead to trouble.

Standing by himself, the idea of a drink was no longer attractive. It was depressing to think about sitting alone knowing that he would end up examining the world from a distance with only the usual cerebral obsession for company. It would be more sensible to go back to the hotel. There, he might be alone but at least there would be a television to keep him occupied. Room service would surely be adequate.

He walked along slowly. The pavement was empty now that the queue had gone but the door to the theatre was still open. On impulse he asked the attendant if any tickets were available.

"Not for sale," the skinny doorman said.

God realised it had been a silly idea. Not every whim would bring a reward.

"This is the BBC, sir, so admission is free. If you'll hang on, I'll check whether there are late returns."

God was speechless. This could only mean that fate wasn't settled and optimism was a reasonable option. Just as well otherwise nobody would make an effort.

"You're in luck, sir. Seats are vacant because there were rumours about a tube strike. Come this way, please."

God stepped inside with hope in his heart. It was clear that his luck had changed. He wondered what the performance would be like. Television is one thing, but how can you see radio? He hoped he would be able to follow.

The show was about to start and God took the first chair he could find. Scattered applause began and a russet haired gentleman, looking remarkably like a schoolboy, walked on to introduce the show. By now God was more adept at following the rituals of behaviour and he watched for clues about when to clap and what was humorous. Nobody laughed at the appearance of the people on stage although they were indeed an odd-looking bunch. It was what they said that mattered. Radio was something he could come to appreciate.

The audience listened as questions were directed to each contestant in turn. There was no sound until the answers started and then it was a free-for-all, laughter and applause rippling around the theatre even when there was little trace of humour. The least mention of Miliband sent the audience into a riot of laughter. God didn't see the point and the mockery was unnecessary but nobody else in the audience gave an indication of the slightest qualm.

The chairman was asking a new question.

"Samira, who took the moral high ground to clear his excess baggage?"

"Oh, this is a delightful story."

God waited for the inevitable political reference.

"Heathrow was busy this week and there's nothing like a grand entrance to start an *incognito* trip. Why do these celebs pretend to avoid the public and then insist on making a dramatic entrance? His greatness, this important gentleman…"

God sat up and paid attention. This could be no coincidence and he certainly didn't laugh. His travel plans were supposed to have been completely secret. It couldn't have been a mistake to come through the main arrivals hall. Not even the pimply customs man had realised who he was.

God looked around. Nothing had changed, no-one had noticed him and the spectators weren't finding the comments funny. An air of awkwardness filled the auditorium as the audience realised they were experiencing an editing-out segment.

"Teams, please, we're straying," the boyish chairman suggested petulantly.

"Could this be," another, bald-headed, contestant pushed on quickly. There was no point in prolonging the agony. "This enormous stout bloke. Eastern

78

gentleman, hedge-fund raider. He didn't want to be bothered by photographers and scurrilous journalists like…"

The team of contestants and chairman gestured in unison towards another member of the panel and, for a long moment, no one spoke. The onlookers, ever tuned for a barbed comment, noted and appreciated the effort and rewarded both teams with a burst of energetic applause.

"Correct, for two points."

God didn't know whether to be relieved or mortified. His cautious strategy had held but he was disappointed to find that nobody knew who he was. And to be compared in importance with this fat man was less than flattering.

The questions continued but God couldn't concentrate. His mind was back at the airport. No wonder things had been strange. The programme had been entertaining in its way and his mind drifted into idle speculation. He thought of companionship and of friendship, and an agreeable scenario wafted to the fore. He needed a guide and his taxi driver could help him see the real side of the city. He looked around to find her but she was invisible in the crowd. Unfortunately, it was also easy to imagine her feelings if she realised he had followed her into the theatre.

A comment from the chairman received polite laughter as the programme ended. God was sitting near the back so it was easy to get away. At the pavement, he turned smartly to the left and made his way to the little church to get his bearings.

The steps of All Souls had been worn down by countless visitors and he wondered how many had been seeking refuge like him. The anonymity of the big city set him free. In Heaven he would have been under constant scrutiny but down here he could do what he liked and nobody would care. Or perhaps one would care if she knew what he was thinking. Come to think of it, her partner would care too. What could he say about himself anyway? He'd want to tell the truth but the story of his experiences would be unbelievable no matter how kind and understanding she was. A fantasy might be pleasant, he might enjoy himself, but in the end he would have to go back to Heaven.

CHAPTER ELEVEN

GOD WATCHED AS THE THEATRE EMPTIED. PEOPLE trickled out through the open doors and, to avoid detection, he stood back in the shadows near the main entrance to the church narrowly missing one of the sleeping men. She appeared after a few minutes, walking arm-in-arm with her companion as they headed towards Regent Street. He waited to give them time to make their way.

It was a beautiful evening, still warm, and the pavements were filled with people. Cars playing music passed nearby on the street. The business of begging had shut down for the day and groups of young men huddled together clutching cans of beer. They made no demands on the passers-by who in turn ignored the sidewalk drinkers. Everybody was getting on with their lives.

God made sure it was safe before he came out of hiding. There was no sign of anyone he recognised and he set off cautiously in search of a place to eat. The programme had been exhausting. If he hadn't been at the airport, he wouldn't have been able to follow anything. All part of being a foreigner, he supposed. As usual, there was an impressive choice; Turkish kebabs, American hamburgers next door to a pizzeria, even an Indian restaurant. A few minutes later he found himself at Oxford Circus. Another famous tourist attraction but it was simply a traffic intersection as far as he could see. Where did English people eat?

Finding nowhere suitable, he decided to go back to the hotel. It had been an emotional day and he was overloaded with experiences as he retraced his way along the broad sidewalk towards the church. The spire was lit from the base and the rough stone looked striking against the smoothness of a deepening blue sky. Across the road, the hotel wasn't particularly attractive but it had been built for capacity rather than for splendour. After everything that had happened over the past few hours, a touch of blandness would do nicely. He made his way slowly, deep in thought, a flicker of movement to one side caught his eye.

"Excuse me..." a man was waving and calling from the Turkish restaurant.

God looked up. And realised with rising panic that the very people he had been avoiding were seated at a table on the pavement. He must have walked past them without noticing.

A range of possible responses flashed through God's mind, foremost was the instinct to press on and pretend he hadn't noticed. Unfortunately, the partner was now standing beside the table waiting for him to respond.

"I…" God hesitated.

"If you're not busy, sir, maybe you would like to join us?" the young man had a surprisingly deep voice.

God waited for his taxi driver to speak but she was staring at the tablecloth. Even from a distance it was obvious she was embarrassed.

"Thank you but I'm on my way back to my hotel," he made his decision. Surely this must be the correct course of action. He turned, ready to be on his way.

"Benjamin!" the driver spoke sternly to her companion and then looked up to speak to God. "I am so sorry. My son loves to make mischief. Please don't let us keep you from your plans."

Definite as her manner may have been, there was no disguising the love between them. The words sounded like rejection but she was smiling and the signals were difficult for God to read. Perhaps it would have been easier if he'd had more practice as a man.

"In that case, I'll wish you a good evening," God replied. Whatever her intention, it was better to err on the side of caution.

He walked away, unable to avoid regret at the missed opportunity. He would have liked to meet her properly and the surprise that the young fellow was her son was palpable. Then again, as he well knew, all sons have fathers.

When he reached the corner, he could disguise a backward glance as caution before he crossed the road. The individual action might seem unimportant but it would be a moment of truth. If she were looking… His expectations had nothing to do with god-liness. Professional rejection would have been easy to bear but he found himself wishing for more in his brief life than he was strictly entitled to. She didn't know who he was so, if she liked him, it meant she was truly interested. This time it be would be personal.

He looked back. She was deep in conversation with the boy and even God couldn't make out an encouraging sign.

"Oh well, nothing ventured nothing gained," he caught himself thinking aloud. It was time to go back to the hotel. He would eat in the room and have a good rest. The next few days would be busy but he had no particular plans. Once he was organised he could contact Gabriel to see if anything urgent had come up in his absence.

He looked towards the hotel. In his heart of hearts he knew communication would show him to be desperate. Nothing could have happened in Heaven after only one day and Gabriel was probably wondering how long he would hold out. Luckily the whole enterprise was secret otherwise the angels would be running a sweepstake.

CHAPTER TWELVE

As GOD WAITED TO CROSS THE ROAD, THE REALISATION dawned that something inexplicable had happened. Before the start of this increasingly strange holiday, a simple thought had been sufficient to summon Gabriel. God may have ignored one or other particular but, had he chosen, any detail would have been at his disposal. He was well aware of the criticisms but omnipotence and omniscience had always been a part of being in charge.

God didn't feel quite so powerful now. Standing on the pavement of an ordinary street, his thoughts were occupied only with personal experiences. Not a single image came to mind even when he turned his attention directly to Heaven. No angels, no flowing robes. The best he could manage was a man in a dressing gown concentrating on a game of chess. He was determined to forget the close encounter with the taxi driver and his mind latched onto the new, more manageable problem. The best option would be to pop back home to make sure everything was all right. It had been irresponsible to leave without making proper arrangements.

"Gabriel," he called quietly. There was no need to make a fuss.

There was no answer, not even a simple sign. A fire-engine, siren blaring, raced down the road on its way to another emergency. A physical reminder, if one were needed, that this place was a long way from Heaven.

"Worldly problems require worldly solutions," God bent his mind to the task. He was, on this journey, a man like any other. The church! It was an obvious answer. God may not have kept up with every development but nobody could forget that this country favoured an established religion. All Souls and the Church of England – God was almost smiling at the thought – the spire was a beacon, a reminder that there was hope.

The chapel was quiet and he took a few deep breaths to gather his thoughts before pushing on the door. Which failed to budge. With mounting irritation, he put his shoulder to the heavy wood and pressed again, still with no success. There were no written instructions but he remembered a similar difficulty at the chicken restaurant in Camden earlier in the day. He tried both ways, pushing, pulling, turning the handle this way and that. The small side entrance was also locked. He returned to the main door and hammered as loudly as he could to attract the attention of someone, anyone, who could help.

"Give it a rest!"

Not registering the disrespectful tone, God looked around. All he understood was that somebody had responded to his call.

"Matey, if you carry on like that, the alarms will go off and the police will take you and us away. We're perfectly comfortable where we are. If you want to make trouble, do it somewhere else."

God searched for the source of the voice. It came from outside the church.

"Where are you?" he asked.

There was a stirring at the end of the loggia from the sleeping bags in the corner. God remembered the men arranging their cardboard boxes earlier in the evening. Clearly he could expect no help. A locked church? He would have something to say about that, at least when he could have his say. There was nothing to do except make his way back to the hotel.

Using the telephone for the first time, he called room service to order a sandwich and sat down to watch television. In due course he would speak to

Gabriel but his last thought as he slipped into sleep was of chicken and a glass of cold beer. He woke in his chair with a start... three o'clock in the morning. The television was still on and pictures drifted across the screen, proof that the world continued without the need for guidance.

God was too exhausted for anything more. With only a vague course of action in mind, he climbed into bed leaving life's obstacles to be dealt with in the morning. Heaven was a distant problem and it didn't take long before he found himself dreaming. Gabriel made no appearance but God was happy with his fantasy of families on Primrose Hill. The only shadows on the landscape were shaped by sunlight filtering through trees as green as any he could imagine.

CHAPTER THIRTEEN

GOD WOKE EARLY. AN UNSUCCESSFUL ATTEMPT TO contact Heaven confirmed the awkwardness of his position and he took breakfast in his room to avoid the chattering of tourists in the public restaurant.

The situation was undoubtedly serious although exactly what had caused the dislocation wasn't clear. Maybe Gabriel wasn't able to respond. It was easy to assign blame but it was also reasonable to suppose that angels derived power from God's presence. In that case, Gabriel would be unable to fulfil his duties and unless there was a positive sign of some sort, God would be left with no choice. He'd have to cut short the holiday and go back to deal with matters himself.

Strangely, he was feeling buoyant, as if he were on the verge of something significant. He ignored the computer and fax on the table in the corner of his bedroom and decided to use a familiar method that could be relied on to produce results. As he had concluded before, in England this must mean the church. Amongst the matters he would be asking

Gabriel to deal with was their practice of locking the doors during the hours of darkness. People might find themselves in trouble at inconvenient times and help should be available. The recollection gave him pause for thought. How could he be sure All Souls would be open when he arrived this morning? That was a bridge to be crossed in due course. If the building were closed, he would simply have to go elsewhere. No wonder people were turning away from religion in droves.

As if in response to his concern, the big blue doors were open and a bright banner welcomed worshippers from any background. At the top of the steps, near where the homeless men had slept, a prominently placed noticeboard advertised a list of forthcoming services. God realised the mystery of organised religion might hide a multitude of details of the team's enthusiastic organisation and he took his place in the sparse congregation without complaint. Personal communication would have been preferable but while on Earth he must take advantage of every normality as it would appear to Heaven.

It would have been easier to make contact on a Tuesday or Wednesday once the weekend's backlog had been dealt with but there was no point worrying about that now and he stayed on afterwards to send a direct message. Even if Gabriel were busy, this unusual conversation would be flagged up as noteworthy because it wasn't part of the routine.

His duty was done and God sat back feeling content. The pace of the response was never in the hands of the supplicant and he could relax for a few hours until he had an answer. After all the stress and worry, at last there was time to see the sights. The only complication was that he had left the travel guide in his room along with the documents and all his money. The satisfaction of only moments earlier evaporated in an instant. Challenges that should have been exciting filled him with the simple fear of failure. He summoned steely resolve but instead had to deal with a rising tide of worry. He must safeguard his belongings. Only then could he think about discovering the streets of London.

After a detour back to the hotel, he set off on the journey of exploration. Starbucks on Langham Place turned out to be the perfect setting to gather his thoughts and, at a quiet table, he made a final check of his possessions. The briefcase, not quite appropriate for a holiday, was turning out to be useful and practical in ways he hadn't imagined. Passport, cash and credit card. All he needed was a cup of coffee to establish his right to occupy a seat.

As he had come to expect, the world, designed to be simple, demonstrated a delight in complications. God's simple request for a drink was met with an amused if friendly reception.

"Diet, decaf, skinny and wet." After a few brief questions, the barista settled on an enigmatic order.

God, as the customer, nodded his acceptance.

"Can I ask your name?"

"Godfrey," he replied quickly, and waited to see if the surname he had chosen would bring a favourable response. In this informal world, it wasn't clear what they would ask for next. If an address were needed, he would have to use the hotel.

"Pleased to meet you, Godfrey," the young man said. The bushy beard was as incongruous as the shaven head and metal piercings that decorated an open, smiling face.

"Thank you," God managed to say. Wet coffee? Skinny? When he got home, he would have to explain when he asked for breakfast. Those putti wouldn't understand anything at all.

God took the cup to his table at the window and sat watching pedestrians passing on the other side of the glass. The drink was fine but he couldn't escape the niggling thought that he should be making more effort to resolve his problem. This time, he thought, why not try somewhere else? There were other churches nearby although it may be better to try somewhere different like a mosque. Feeling efficient, he popped open the case and paged through the guide book to find a map. Closest would be... He was delighted to see a synagogue nearby, probably as good even if it were Friday. It would be only a few minutes walk on the back streets behind the BBC.

What he wanted, most of all, was to avoid creating the impression of being desperate. The call to Gabriel must be simply to alert Heaven to the possibility of a difficulty. No-one else need be told. God would deal with the situation and was checking-in to make sure they were all right.

CHAPTER FOURTEEN

GOD LOOKED INTO THE WINDOWS AS HE FOLLOWED THE route to the local synagogue. It was mid-morning and every one of the shops was open. A bank, sandwiches, artificial fires and office furniture. The assortment was endless, with a series of restaurants and public houses planted strategically on every corner. Even at this early hour people were drinking. Men and women, glasses of beer in hand, occupied the pavements and spilled into the road with nonchalant contempt for the approaching traffic. He walked on, determined not to be distracted.

The synagogue was on a quiet street with stained-glass windows protected by a metal grille. It was lucky God hadn't allowed his hopes to gather too much momentum. The building was closed and a board fixed to the door listed a schedule of services almost identical to All Souls church. He couldn't help but feel disappointed. Once upon a time, there had been great differences between the old religions whereas now they were recognisable only by the times they prayed. And that was an administrative convenience for the sake of Heaven.

Turning away from the desolation of a traditional outlet, he was more than a little surprised to find a welcoming establishment next door. In a demonstration of consequence and efficiency, the grand temple of the General Medical Council was open to all. Thinking back to the life he had left behind, God recalled that the group proclaimed independence and eschewed traditional connections. They may be open but on this of all days he needed something more.

The decision about his next move was easy to make. God chose relevance over proximity and picked out the fastest route to St Paul's Cathedral. He was in a hurry and the head office of worship and prayer in England would be the best option in the middle of a confusing day. If everything went well, there would be time enough afterwards to do something interesting.

There was so much to learn, God reflected, as he waited in line to buy a ticket at Oxford Circus Tube station. He was still carrying the briefcase and in his suit looked much like any other insurance broker or businessman on a normal day at work. Directions to St Paul's were easy. God thanked the attendant and allowed pressure from the crowd to direct him forward. With a day-pass firmly in hand, the barriers presented no problems and he stepped gingerly onto an escalator that led down into the bowels of the Earth. There was no chance of turning back and he tried not to think about Heaven, the airiness and open spaces, telling himself all would be fine once he had made it to his final destination.

He looked up at the notification signal on a board above the platform. Seven minutes until the arrival of the next train.

The environment was grey and gloomy with nothing to distract attention beyond a profusion of advertisements for telephones, whisky and foreign holidays. God walked away from the few other prospective passengers and peered into the blackness of the tunnel while he waited for time to pass. With nothing to do, he was forced to look inwards. It was no great metaphorical leap from the colourless station to the state of affairs that awaited when he reached the other side. There was nothing to light his way and he couldn't be sure of the direction in which the train would run. If life is a circle, as some of those mystics were so fond of insisting, then it wouldn't matter at all. God, on the other hand, was a believer in progress and improvement. There would be no purpose to creation if everything had been done before and would inevitably come around again. It was a thought that led him to realise that he was more interested in the future than in the past. He couldn't help smiling, the debate going backwards and forwards in his head. It's all very well to be interested but it's a different matter knowing what to do. The future is precisely that which can't be seen; on the other hand, the only way of looking forward is to hold the past firmly in view.

He paced a little more energetically in the private corner of his platform. With very little effort he had managed to get himself smartly out of the conundrum and it was now possible to look into the tunnel with new eyes. It didn't matter which way he was facing, both ways led towards the future. He may have lost some of his powers but he still had the authority of reason. Anyway the explanation was obvious. A red light positioned on the wall at one end told the driver where to stop. So he had that figured out too.

More and more people were arriving. The information sign still suggested a seven minute wait and the gloom of the tunnel remained impenetrable. God forced his mind towards more pleasant visions and his re-invigorated imagination obliged with vistas of Heaven looking remarkably similar to Primrose Hill. Repeated setbacks could be disheartening and he had begun to doubt himself but whatever happened now he knew that his mind would always come to the rescue. Resourcefulness is no small thing.

It was a pleasing exercise in arbitrary thought and one which dragged God towards the moment of arrival. The rails had begun vibrating, emitting a pleasing musical sound: *Train Approaching* appeared on the notice board. He grasped the briefcase so that it wouldn't be left behind and regarded the tunnel one last time. There was a light, coming ever closer. It was possible to stretch an allegory too far but there was no benefit to be gained by ignoring a hopeful sign. He would certainly have been depressed if there had been a delay and he was entitled to make use of an encouraging signal if that's what the world had to offer.

A wave of air announced the train's appearance and God climbed aboard waiting anxiously until his transport stuttered into motion. If the next station were Tottenham Court Road, everything would be all right. The walls of the tunnel rushed past outside the window. Soon enough he would be at St. Paul's Cathedral. If he were going to re-establish contact, this would certainly be the place to do it.

The train sped on, pausing briefly at Holborn and Chancery Lane, and God made ready for the forthcoming stop. Nervous as he had been at the start of the expedition, the underground was hardly intimidating. The carriage was filled to bursting with an effervescent cocktail of travellers; surpisingly, not one spoke on a mobile phone.

The doors opened and God was ready, eager for the next stage of his journey. The *Way Out* was clearly signposted and he felt a sense of anticipation akin to redemption as an escalator carried him upward. Inevitably, he experienced a twinge as he approached the barrier but the gates responded to his ticket and opened to let him through.

CHAPTER FIFTEEN

ST PAUL'S CHURCH WAS LESS INSPIRING UP CLOSE than had been suggested by the picture in the guide book. It was large and imposing but in a curious state of disrepair. God reminded himself about the lesson of the radio quiz and tried not to be swayed by appearances. On the other hand, he thought, the purpose of a structure must be linked to its external form otherwise for what purpose had beauty been created? He decided to think these questions through if he ever had to spend time underground again, although that was hardly likely.

From the tube station he walked through a shaded garden. There were many small doors set into the stone walls but, like every other church, this cathedral was sure to have an imposing entrance. It wasn't long before he found what he was looking for. A queue had formed at the top of a grand bank of steps so God waited to one side and took the opportunity to gather his thoughts. The square at the front was filled with people but something was incongruous.

Like a little brother trying to imitate an older sibling, the scene was designed to imitate the Vatican but the weather was wrong and English people were too busy. The pigeons were another eyesore, as drab and dirty as everything else.

At the first few drops of rain, he turned to go inside. The entrance was blocked by a gate, which explained why there had been a queue.

"Surely not!" a gasp of astonishment escaped as he entered the final doorway. Visitors had to pay. Had they forgotten this behaviour had been proscribed for nearly two millennia? Prayer should be free at the point of delivery. Even the most modern of medical people, he had been assured, understood the importance of the decision. A logjam built up as he struggled with the briefcase to find his wallet.

"What happens to somebody who can't afford the fee?" he asked the money collector.

"It's not up to me. I'm only doing my job," the man was wearing a dark blazer and tie, a grim expression of disinterest fixed in position on his face.

"Well, who makes these decisions? I think it's appalling," God saw no reason to hold back. Opinions like these should have force on Earth as they did in Heaven. "A house of religion should be open to all.

102

Not only people who are rich."

"No use telling me, elegant sir," the man said with exaggerated courtesy. "You can make your complaint any time you like but if you want to go in you'll have to pay £18 like everybody else."

"£18!" God spluttered. "That would feed a family for a week."

"Much as I would love to debate the ins-and-outs of modern capitalism, there are other visitors who would appreciate it if you would make your decision," for some reason the gatekeeper had begun smiling. He reached for a printed sheet protected in laminated plastic, fixed a pair of reading glasses in place and declaimed in a sing-song voice. "Here begins the lesson: *Entrance fees are set by the Council...* I'm not reading all that nonsense, it's a complete waste of time. If you want to come in, you contribute. Otherwise you can pray outside."

The man ended his speech with a look of satisfaction designed to make God's blood boil. Behind him, in the queue, there were protests at the delay.

"I want a receipt," God said, trying to break through the wall of smugness.

"You'll get a ticket like everybody else. I'm sure you can use that to claim on your expense account."

What could all this possibly mean? Not for the first time since arriving in London, God felt he had missed some vital point. The feeling of powerlessness was alarming but it was clear he had no choice. Of one thing he was certain – there would be consequences. The Church may not know who he was now, but they would. As soon as he got back to Heaven.

St Paul's was more of a museum than a working house of prayer and was properly open for business on only special occasions. God struggled to find signs of worship. A few tourists examined displays but not many were interested in relics of the past. History was dull and uninviting, like a rural bus stop *en route* to the big bright terminus that was today. Then, as he had discovered for himself earlier, the future couldn't be examined in any practical way at all, which meant people found themselves confined to the present. Being pragmatic creatures, most were happy with their lot, except the unfortunate visitors who followed their pre-set route until it was time to go home. So much for criticism. God knew that if he had been similarly organised, a small private plane could have been waiting at Heathrow to take him home.

He set himself down under the dome where he was unlikely to be disturbed. It was time to get the exercise started.

"Huhmmph," God cleared his throat. It was more difficult putting thoughts into words than he had imagined and it was disconcerting to be dealing with intimate matters in a public place. A quick look around confirmed that nobody was watching. He closed his eyes and tried to concentrate as the sound of voices drifted across the open space.

Our father who art in Heaven...

If only they knew. God weighed up his options but he could see why a fixed format might be comforting. Most people didn't want much from their prayers anyway. Usually they were after a little reassurance and encouragement to press ahead. He, on the other hand, had a definite request to get across.

"Gabriel?" he whispered, gradually overcoming his embarrassment. If anyone looked, they would see a man sitting quietly with his head bowed in concentration. Nothing at all inappropriate. "I find myself in a little difficulty and I need to talk to you. Urgently. Things have not gone to plan."

The problem with visualisation persisted. He could manage a landscape well enough but the team he needed to contact remained out of focus. He leaned forward one more time.

"Can you hear me? I'm in Paul's church, London. Get back to me as soon as possible. I'll wait as long as I can, after that…" After that, he wasn't sure what to do. They could be dealing with an emergency but it was probably the usual Friday cacophony with so many people trying to have their say.

A tour party gathered nearby, the guide pointing out architectural features with no mention of faith or conviction. God moved to a quieter position and waited for a sign to materialise. Why did everything keep going wrong? The whole place remained dry and lifeless.

"This is God calling with a message for Gabriel," he checked his watch. "It's Friday afternoon and I'm waiting under the dome."

What else could he say? If only he had one of those little telephones.

"… I can also be contacted at the Heritage Hotel near Regent Street. I'm registered under the name *Godfrey*. I look forward to hearing from you as soon as possible."

God considered his position. The formality of the words should alert Gabriel to the urgency of the situation without giving any lesser angel cause for concern. There was nothing left to do but hope.

★

After a brief turn on the square where he managed to buy lunch, God realised he would have to go back inside. Something might have happened although Gabriel could easily have manifested in the teashop or on the steps where he ate his sandwich. Aside from the weight of history, there wasn't much difference between a café and a cathedral. He tossed the remnants of food into a waste bin and took up his briefcase, striding confidently to the barred entrance.

The money collector smirked at him.

"That will be £18."

"I've paid," God said impatiently.

"Well, now, let me see... I do remember the face. You've been in before but you'll have to pay again. The price is the same and you only get to go in once. Next time, book online and you'll get a discount for an annual pass." There was no queue to distract them and the man was quivering with satisfaction.

"No," God spoke firmly, struggling not to lose his temper. "I went outside for fresh air and it's patently unfair for anyone to have to pay twice." He leaned on the gate to force it open.

From inside the church, a man in a flowing robe reminiscent of Heaven was taking an interest in the argument. He stood watching from the nave and gave the impression that he was deciding whether to intervene.

"Just a moment, just a moment," God's persecutor had a hand on the barrier and was using his strength to keep it closed. "I don't know who you think you are but you can't expect special treatment."

"Can I be of assistance?" To prevent the argument escalating further, the man with the pious air moved forward. He was evidently a person of authority; the money changer had turned back to his seat looking pale and a little nervous.

"I paid to come in earlier," God said quickly, fumbling for the ticket. "Please, I need to go inside."

"That's reasonable. What do you think, John?"

The barrier opened and God pushed through. He didn't stop to consider the minor victory and hurried towards his original seat. There was no sign at all and he sank to his knees with his head on the back of the pew in front. It looked like he might have to wait until after the weekend. There was no option except to go back to the hotel. At least that was constant and dependable.

The saintly man watched from the side until God had finished praying. Most visitors were tourists so perhaps it was justifiable to ask for money but it should be different when someone came in for religious reasons. He waited patiently; the way people attended to their spiritual needs was nobody's business but their own.

God was taken aback to see his rescuer waiting. He had been looking for positive signs but a priest with an offer of a refund wasn't exactly what he had been expecting. Nevertheless, he was pleased to speak to someone about his problems and comforted by the assurances. John had a difficult history, the clergyman explained, and this wasn't the first time such an incident had taken place. Supervision and retraining had already been arranged.

God was pleased to find a demonstration of goodness and his anger evaporated. Nevertheless, he considered it important to voice his concerns about the entrance fee, even for people on a simple holiday.

"You are right, sir, of course, but we have to live in this world," the apologist smiled wanly. "Sometimes unpalatable things are forced on us. It's the same when employees misbehave. There are labour laws. We may want to take action but sometimes we are constrained by circumstances beyond our control."

Knowing the complications that must be dealt with by any organisation, God forbore from forcing home his point. He didn't mind making a contribution, it was the coercion that had distressed him.

The insight settled matters for the day. The weary priest was undoubtedly doing his best and the assistance God needed would have to come from a higher source. As for earthly matters, he knew about the footbridge to the Tate Modern and that entrance would be free. There would be time enough to think about art and the niceties of life once he had solved the mystery of the disappearance of Heaven. Today, he wasn't in the mood for frivolity and he set off for the hotel on foot. Never mind that it was raining.

CHAPTER SIXTEEN

THE PAVEMENT, WHICH HAD BEEN DRAB AND DIRTY, WAS now drab and wet. The rain was pouring down but God hardly noticed. He was distracted and walked on automatically, stopping only occasionally to get his bearings. Progress was slow as he followed main roads thinking of safety and his final objective. First along Fleet Street, past Trafalgar Square and finally up Regent Street towards the hotel.

He arrived at his destination in a bedraggled state. The rain had found its way around his umbrella and his mood was in sharp contrast to the smiling faces of employees determined to provide an enthusiastic welcome.

"Oh dear, Mr Godfrey, you must take care… No, I'm sorry, we haven't received any messages."

God handed over the umbrella and nodded his thanks before making his way upstairs as soon as possible.

The bedroom was large and comfortable, furnished with every facility. He dried his clothes with the hairdryer and checked that the briefcase had turned out to be waterproof. As he was looking at his money, he noticed he hadn't signed the back of the credit card. The receptionist, downstairs, must have overlooked that too when he first arrived.

He hunted around for a pen and copied the signature from the passport to ensure both matched, then looked for something more to do. There was no sound in the room except from the fax machine humming quietly in the corner. SmartFax, the label said. Plainly a false promise because the machine did nothing and said nothing at all useful. On the other hand, God couldn't help thinking, the sound, unvarying and uniform, was an accurate reflection of his prospects for the rest of the day.

In his boredom, he pressed the buttons randomly listening to the tones from the keypad before trying to play a tune. He gave up after a few moments whereupon the machine coughed and spluttered into life. There was a whirring sound and paper emerged. With a letter! For him!

MEMORANDUM REPORT.
TRANSMISSION FAILED.
UNABLE TO DETECT OUTGOING COPY.
PLEASE RE-INSERT AND TRY AGAIN.

It was a false alarm; still it brought the beginnings of an idea. While he waited, he could chivvy Gabriel along with a note. There was no harm trying anyway. All he needed was a number and to write the message. He found some paper and spelled out his instruction, making sure it was short and to the point. And since he was using the hotel's letterhead, Gabriel would get contact details for the hotel.

        **GABRIEL COMMA THIS IS GOD STOP
        CALL IMMEDIATELY STOP**

The number was easy to find, it was almost the first listing in the phone directory. Emergencies: 999

Without further ado, he inserted his page, pressed the digits and selected **SEND**. The machine whirled into action and the message reappeared on a lower tray with the added bonus of a confirmation slip. The mechanism functioned like clockwork.

After years of reluctance, God examined the fax with friendlier eyes. If the machine worked, if it got him back to Heaven, he would be a convert. He pictured his office as it soon might be with new lines for telephones, everybody with a computer tucked under his or her arm. A bit like London today, only cleaner. He was sure there would be coffee.

With nothing left to do, his thoughts were growing ever more fantastical. Room service was helpful and he could always be distracted by food but Gabriel might not call for a day or two and he could hardly wait all that time indoors. What he needed was one of those little telephones so that he would be contactable anywhere. Technology could set him free.

The confinement would soon be over and he took up his briefcase with a muted feeling of elation. His mood must have showed because the young receptionist smiled as she offered directions for Oxford Street and advice about mobile phones. He set off, not even bothering to take an umbrella.

The choice on offer provided the usual challenge. Every shop was bright and inviting, the atmosphere of excitement was infectious and God examined the tiny instruments while he waited in the queue. It wasn't long before his turn arrived. He explained what he wanted. Messages, of course, and telephone calls. The salesman took him through the options. God was bewildered.

"Could I get a phone and look at the choices

later?" he asked cautiously.

The adviser sighed inwardly but knew he had to make allowances. At least the old gent was trying.

"Not really. You need to have a handset and a line rental." He paused, noticing the look on his customer's face. "The handset is the actual telephone."

"Which one will bring messages fastest?" God asked, relieved to have a sympathetic helper.

"They're all much the same. The companies send messages instantaneously."

God knew this wasn't true, couldn't be. All that was important was that they were identical.

The adviser took the pause for agreement and continued.

"You can choose from O_2, EE, Vodafone. Orange has rebranded."

"I'm not worried about the colour," God interjected. The process was more difficult than he had anticipated and he didn't want the added complication of having to deal with aesthetics.

"It's nothing like that, sir," the adviser smiled. "Orange is the name of a company. Well, it was until… never mind, that's probably not important."

"I see. Thank you," God was embarrassed but decided to press on. "I'd like a phone that I can use anywhere, on a train too, you understand. Which would you recommend?"

After much to-ing and fro-ing, the choice was made. God would have a contract and a bright little device that would give him not only phone calls but also a mailbox, messages and the internet. That was something to be considered in the future. Then, finally, the matter of payment. God reached for his wallet and counted out his notes.

"I'm sorry, sir, but if you want a contract we'll need your account details so that your bill can be paid every month. And I'll have to run a credit check," the salesman said.

Luckily God had brought the credit card, understandably essential in these modern times.

"I don't think I explained properly. We need your bank details and another form of identification," the young fellow was eager to get to the end.

"My passport?" God asked, reaching for his briefcase.

"That's a start but we need a document with your home address, like a gas bill or a council-tax letter. Anything like that will do."

God had a sinking feeling. Everything in this place was so convoluted. He had offered proper money. Why didn't they want to help?

"Couldn't you charge my credit card in advance?" he asked.

"If you want a contract then I'm sorry, no…"

God turned and fled. He couldn't bear the frustration any longer. How was he to make progress if the answer was always no?

★

"What was that about?" the manager of the store asked. He had a series of stars on his lapel denoting authority and there was nothing he hadn't seen.

"I don't know. I spent nearly an hour going through everything and then he didn't have documents."

"Maybe you could have given him a pre-paid phone," the senior figure suggested. Everybody had to learn. The young chap was new and was taking the situation to heart. "These older men are often complicated. Women are much more practical."

"I was about to suggest other options but he ran out. As if…" the salesman petered into silence. "He spoke good English but I don't think he was local."

"Win some, lose some," the manager gave his new recruit a friendly pat on the shoulder.

"Yep."

CHAPTER SEVENTEEN

IT FELT LIKE A CONSPIRACY AS GOD HURRIED BACK along Oxford Street towards the only place that was safe. The hotel was now more than simply a place to rest and eat. It had become the centre of his existence and the focal point for his attempts to escape. He needed time to think.

"I'm sorry, Mr Godfrey, no messages yet," the receptionist was still on duty. "Did you have any luck at the shops? I'm due for an upgrade soon, what did you go for?"

"I... ah... decided against a telephone. But thank you for your advice," his difficulties were impossible to explain. He excused himself and headed for his room.

Everything about this life seemed incomprehensible. Lying on the bed, drifting in the orbit of his thoughts, God revisited the revelation that his lost powers derived from the position he had once occupied in Heaven. The idea didn't leave him despondent mainly because of the corollary that everything would be back to normal when he returned to his rightful place. All he had to do was get back. Then, turning a corner in his contemplations, he realised that if status came from being in charge then he wasn't special at all. Gabriel must have wanted to take his place permanently otherwise God would have found himself summoned back to Heaven. In which case he would be Himself all over again? It was too confusing to fathom and he drifted into sleep.

The world felt different when he awoke. He dressed for dinner and ate in the dining room accompanied by his book and a bottle of wine. From now on he would make the most of his free time instead of worrying and making plans. He wasn't the only one eating alone so there was no need to feel awkward.

Saturday came. The weather was a distracting mixture of rain and sunshine but God pressed on with the task of contacting Heaven. There were any number of religious outlets to visit and it was a pleasant surprise to find that people could be colourful and entertaining when they were given the chance. He had considered seeing a lawyer but, like doctors, it was difficult to get an appointment on the weekend, a clear sign they were outside Heaven's circle.

A pattern of habits had developed and with it came a degree of contentment and security. The following day would be Sunday and he would rest. If he were recalled on Monday, he didn't want the last day to have been wasted.

The future settled, he retired to his room, reassured by warm thoughts about the inevitable resurrection. This time he dreamed his bed was transported to Heaven and ushered through Peter's gate with a flourish and a fanfare. Tantalisingly, Gabriel made no appearance but that hardly detracted from a triumphant return after days spent battling bureaucracy on Earth. Pleasant dreams and God slept on, protected by the relics of a self-image and hopes so powerful they could almost have been real.

Sunday passed uneventfully. There was an unfamiliar face at the reception desk when he stopped to ask about messages on his way to the restaurant in the evening. The request was as much a part of his routine as anything else that happened in the hotel.

"Sir, what time will you be checking out?"

The pocket of the new receptionist's jacket was decorated with flags of the world. He looked down respectfully and waited for his customer to speak. God glanced around, there was nobody else in the foyer. The question had been addressed to him.

"I beg your pardon?" God said.

"Your reservation was for five nights and I think ...

yes, you were supposed to be leaving on Monday, which is tomorrow," the man offered hesitantly. As the only member of staff at the front desk he had a duty not to panic but it was less than a week since his transfer from Shanghai. There had been warnings at home about the complications he might encounter when dealing with clients in famous London and he resolved to do his best.

"Sir, there is no difficulty if you plan to be with us longer. I am sending immediately a message to booking desk. Please, I apologise for a most grave error." He gave a bow and, in an expression of oriental courtesy, waited again for the guest to speak.

"Thank you," God managed to mumble and turned away to hide his face. Of course he wanted to stay. It was the only reasonable thing to do. He had nowhere else to go and he was expecting an important communication. "Please, send the message. Thank you, I'm sure that will be best."

At least he had managed to maintain his temper, God searched for crumbs of comfort. There had been a time when he would have thrown a fit and caused a ruckus, shouting at everybody even if it weren't their fault. A recollection of the day of arrival resurfaced, the plan for a small hotel and idyllic mornings in a café with banter over breakfast. Those simple expectations had turned out to be less than practical and he was determined to stay in the hotel, this hotel, for as long as it was required. He had cash and he had credit, in fact he had every right to extend his stay.

Eventually he remembered that nobody was arguing. The booking desk would deal with the request and that would be that. In any case, as he knew from a few days in the city, there were hundreds of hotels. If they didn't want him here, he would take his custom somewhere else.

CHAPTER EIGHTEEN

IT WAS MONDAY MORNING AND GOD WAS FEELING confident. The weekend, always busy in Heaven, was over and Gabriel would soon be in contact. He had to be patient but of one thing he was certain – there would be no going back to the day when everybody had felt obliged to say *no* to even the simplest of requests.

He opened the lid of his briefcase and checked the contents quickly. Aside from a dwindling supply of cash, there wasn't much more than his passport, the credit card and a change of underwear bought the previous day in an idle moment. He would need more clothes if there were no news this morning but he felt secure with the hotel as a base. After breakfast he would make sure the reservation had been extended.

"Best to look good when the pressure's on," God thought, humming to himself as the razor glided smoothly over cheek and jowl. Couldn't remember having to shave in Heaven.

The door to his room slammed as he stepped into the corridor on his way to the restaurant and, too late, he realised he had forgotten to pick up the briefcase. He would have to get into the room. Every time he thought he was making progress, some new obstruction reared its head. Forcing the door was not an option but, as with other problems in the world, there was likely to be a solution. He shook his head in disbelief. The solution was obviously an electronic key and his had been left on the table beside his briefcase. He'd have to ask for help. This time there was no alternative.

Without further hesitation, he dashed to the lift. The indicator told him to wait but impatience took over and he tapped again and again on the call button.

"Good morning, sir, to you."

God stopped drumming. A chambermaid was dusting the atrium.

"Morning," he said curtly.

"So many arrival today. Our hotel must be more than full," she continued, barely noticing the guest's mood. This job wasn't much different from looking after a house full of children. Only a few hours and she would be on her way home.

"Can you help me?" he looked at the maid for the first time, a resolution to the latest difficulty materialising in his mind. "I can't get into my room. Do you have a key?"

She must have, he thought, otherwise how could she do the cleaning?

"This can happen many times," she said soothingly. "You go for reception and some girl will help. No need for worry. Ground floor, the lift…"

"Yes, yes, I know that."

Don't be ridiculous, of course he knew how to get to the foyer. Why did she think he was pressing the button? Instead of this nonsense, she should *open the damned door*.

"This is not permitted. People's room is private," she was more than a little shocked. Like children, she had thought earlier, but her girls, five and six years old, were much better behaved.

"Forgive me," God took a deep breath. As usual, when he was irritated, thoughts had found their way audibly to the surface. But he couldn't stop for a proper expression of regret. There would be time to worry about his temper afterwards, once he had managed to reclaim his possessions. "I'll take the stairs. I'm sure it will be quicker."

God made his way down the fire-escape and arrived in the foyer, puffing slightly. Thank goodness, his favourite receptionist was at the desk. He hurried over and she smiled as always.

"Hello there, Mr Godfrey, are you all right?"

"I'm fine," he gathered himself. "I've locked myself out of my room."

"Oh, Mr G, don't worry," she said. "These things happen all the time. I'll get someone to open up for you. Do you want to have breakfast first?"

"Is there any chance you could do it now? I need my briefcase and…"

"And you're worried," she completed the sentence. She called a colleague to take her place and led her anxious guest across the foyer to the lift. "Come on, Mr Godfrey, let's get you sorted out."

What a charming girl – God couldn't help smiling with relief – and so efficient. Within seconds she had the situation under control. The lift arrived without delay and she looked marvellous swinging her pass-card as she walked.

They rounded a corner in the corridor. God's heart skipped a beat. The door to his room was open. Thieves? And he had been gone only five minutes. The chambermaid must have been watching and helped them. She had a key and knew that he had gone downstairs.

"Looks like someone's cleaning your room," the

receptionist's voice broke into his thoughts. "Hello, Maria. I didn't realise you were up here or I would have called to ask you to open up… well, there you are, Mr Godfrey. Let me know if there's anything else we can do."

God could barely speak. The briefcase was on the bedside table, exactly as he had left it. The maid gathered her equipment and edged her way out of the room.

"Would you mind?" God gestured to her to wait. "Please."

"Very sorry I couldn't open, sir, but this is a rule from the hotel," a set of rosary beads had materialised in one hand, nothing could disguise her state of apprehension.

God knew it had been a terrible misjudgement. In times past he had delighted in being vengeful but something more gentle was more appropriate when he was undoubtedly in the wrong.

"It was anxiety," he said. "Please accept my apology. I am sure you did the right thing." Hopefully she didn't realise he had suspected her of stealing.

But she knew what he thought – a servant to be pushed and pulled as he willed and then a touch of contrition to salve the conscience. He may have apologised but she was sorry too. Rich people is the same all over, losing temper over a small type of nothing. So lucky, she thought to herself, imagine if a bad business happened.

She excused herself. She would come back later to finish cleaning when she wasn't in the way.

He took his seat in the dining room and got breakfast underway. Under normal circumstances the ritual would have been comforting as he relaxed and enjoyed the view. Unfortunately, the more he thought about the morning's debacle, the worse it appeared to be.

In retrospect, he had been over-anxious and should certainly have been more polite. The difficulty was that there was no way of knowing what the maid thought of his apology. Some reparation was due even if she believed him but the rate of exchange between insult and injury was less than clear. There was nothing of substance he could think of and he could only imagine how angry she would be if he proffered money. Alternating between irritation and contrition, he took up his fork, chasing the last piece of bacon around the plate. There was no way out and he couldn't turn the clock back. There was nothing to do except chalk this one up to experience.

Back in the room, God waited out the rest of the morning like a captive in a perfumed prison cell with nothing to do but watch television. Gabriel had still not shown his face and every excuse God could manufacture was wearing thin. The weekend didn't explain anything. What if he really was in trouble, if the hotel burned down or if he had no funds? He made ready to leave remembering that he had forgotten to check on the status of his reservation.

With the briefcase tucked under an arm and the room key in hand for security, he looked around. For all the time he had spent in the bedroom, he had barely made an impression. Apart from an unused suitcase, a disposable razor and an anonymous toothbrush, he wouldn't be leaving any trace. There was one more thing to do before he went down to the reception desk. In the drawer of the desk he found a pen, paper and an envelope.

"I am sorry about my behaviour this morning. Please forgive me," he wrote, and signed the note *God* before considering the name with some surprise. It was an easy slip to make, but equally easily corrected. *Godfrey* would be more suitable.

He folded two banknotes with the letter, sealed the envelope and, finally, he was done.

RESURRECTION

CHAPTER NINETEEN

A NIGHTMARE JOLTED GABRIEL INTO CONSCIOUSNESS but the details were fading as He awoke. Something was wrong. It was His bedroom with the same furnishings and there was the usual choir singing out of sight… the confusion dissipated and He made His way to God's office, waiting in the anteroom while a small army of putti prepared headquarters for the new week. The view through the window across Heaven was incomparable but there was a feeling of strangeness. It was almost as if everything were aligned towards Him as He stood watching from above.

Never mind, He thought, yawning quietly. Sundays were usually busy but yesterday had been more peaceful. What would the next few days bring? He settled into an armchair and rested His feet on a stool. The peculiar sensation persisted. It wasn't quite trepidation because this was Heaven and nothing could go wrong. His mind turned to the administrative tasks waiting to be dealt with. Perhaps

He could ask Michael to lend a hand. A curious rush surrounded the room, a repositioning of…

"Oh!" Gabriel caught his breath. Almost at the same instant, the angel Michael put his head around the door. "Hello, Mike, I was just thinking of you. What's happened? You look terrible. Had a bad weekend?"

"Thank goodness You're here," Michael closed the door and hesitated, uncertain how to proceed. It wasn't long since the last time they'd been waiting together outside the office but that had been before the big temper tantrum when God had offered a promotion. He remembered God saying something about Gabriel being put out to pasture yet the old Archangel was sitting in the anteroom with His aura of power intact, possibly it was even stronger. Almost as though He had taken charge.

"Come in, sit down. Make yourself comfortable," Gabriel said. "Tell Me what's going on. It looks as if you've been up for days."

Michael remembered Gabriel's confrontation with God a few days back. That had taken real guts and he must do his best to follow the example. He would have to be careful. Gabriel had been notoriously even-tempered but it wasn't clear exactly what was going on.

"Forgive me for speaking informally," he offered cautiously. "Do You remember what it was like when You were God's deputy?"

"Of course, it was only last week. How could I forget?" Gabriel said irritably.

Exactly as Michael feared. Gabriel's personality had changed, imperious and impatient, much like His predecessor before the big change. Michael took a deep breath and carried on.

"I'm sorry, I didn't mean to imply… well, You know how busy the weekends can be. So much to do, so little time."

"Yes, yes, I remember all that," Gabriel waved at the youngster to continue. "Interesting times but the system worked, didn't it? Muslims then Jews and Christians, others spread over the week. Anyone could join a fringe group but there was no fast-tracking from beyond the pale. Tell me, why are you so worn out?"

"Things have been getting out of hand," Michael smiled wanly. Telling the story was exactly what he was trying to do.

"My dear chap, I would have helped but I had no idea. Really, you should have let Me know."

"The truth is, Sir…"

"What's got into you, Michael? It's Me, Gabriel.

We've worked together in the past and I don't see... Oh, you've been thinking of God's little idea about shuffling the senior ranks around and now you're afraid I'll be upset. Is that it?"

"Not exactly," Michael wasn't sure how to explain. "When things started going wrong, I tried to contact God but all I got was the old message. You know the one about Sunday being a day of rest? I was so relieved to be summoned, I thought it meant he was back at work."

"He's not available. I'm looking after the office for a few days," Gabriel didn't quite understand. "But there was no summons, I was thinking about getting started and you arrived. A coincidence, that's all."

"Um," Michael had arrived at the point he dreaded most. "If You're taking over, I need... I mean... I'd like to ask for an assistant."

"I'm not taking over," Gabriel laughed. "God's taken a short holiday. It's supposed to be secret so We won't tell anyone else. No idea where he went but he'll be home soon and everything will get back to normal. Sorry about the weekend, though, I'll make it up to you next time."

"It's more serious than You think. There are papers You should see," Michael offered a folder.

"Of course, of course," Gabriel said soothingly. "Let's deal with your problems. We can chat about the vicissitudes of life later."

At last, Michael thought, Lord Gabriel was taking the situation seriously. It had been a busy few days. The usual flood of pleas and complaints that would have been tricky to deal with even if he'd had help. He didn't want to be disrespectful but God was a hard act to follow. No doubt their new Leader would grow into the role but no-one could expect Him to be as surefooted as God, not yet.

"So You'll understand..." Michael said.

"There's no need to explain," Gabriel muttered, the atmosphere in Heaven darkened in correspondence with His mood. "I seem to know exactly what you've been thinking. Very strange."

And the penny dropped.

"If I can do all this... how's he getting on?"

"That's what I'm trying to explain," Michael tried to hold back the feeling of exasperation. "We've been getting very bizarre messages from England. I didn't know what to do, that's why I needed help."

"I see," suddenly Gabriel was completely alert. "Tell Me everything."

"I was dealing with the routine stuff when these

notes started coming in. At first it didn't look very interesting and I had a lot on my plate," Michael felt the weight lifting from his shoulders. "Then things got strange. There was a flurry of messages from someone claiming to be God and every single one of them originated in central London. It could have been nothing but I knew the situation was serious when Paul started bringing memos."

"I suppose you sent an appropriate answer," Gabriel knew what He would have done in Michael's place.

"I've never been in this position before so I didn't know how to start," Michael felt he was going around in circles. "At that stage it was guess work. So far none of the associates has made the connection but it could cause trouble if they find out God's not here."

"You're right," Gabriel thought out loud. "This is something We must keep between Ourselves. Isn't it odd that you couldn't get hold of Me? I don't feel any different."

Michael wasn't sure what to say.

"Never mind," Gabriel realised He needed to take control. He led Michael to the window to see what was happening. "Okay, let's see these notes of yours.

Better still, come with Me. We'd better do something to keep the gossip under control. We'll say that God's involved in a big project. That's happened before so nobody will be surprised."

Gabriel and Michael set off on a brief tour of the dominions. Heaven had been edging towards a collective jitter but seeing two senior colleagues in tandem set the angels at rest and everyone relaxed into the routine of a Monday morning. There was a little excitement about God's new project. Gabriel would have to think of something but that was probably best done later in private. He had a few ideas – the main thing was to keep everybody happy.

It was nearing mid-afternoon when they finished their review and at last sat down to consider God's precarious situation. Michael produced the file with details of his attempts to track the old man down below. He'd done his best and couldn't be blamed for the woeful lack of success.

"I don't suppose there's much point going over everything from the beginning," Gabriel said. He was keen to be getting on and leafed quickly through the records. "Why is it taking so long for messages to get through? Look, these were sent on Friday from All

Souls in Langham Place. And there's one from the same place on Thursday evening… really, Mike, We should have known earlier."

"Let's see," Michael struggled on, not yet familiar with the minutiae of his job. "It looks like on Friday we expect more Islamic prayer so the church notes must have been filed at the bottom of the pile. That's the only thing I can think of. I asked Paul about the delay from that cathedral but he didn't have an explanation."

Gabriel rolled his eyes but allowed Michael to continue.

"Here's the one that really caught my attention. It's a fax. You know how he hated machines so he must have been pretty desperate. The fire brigade treated it as a hoax but our representative thought it looked interesting and passed it on."

"Let's have a look," Gabriel cast an eye over the facsimile sheet. Definitely God's style, terse and to the point. And definitely worth pursuing.

"The Heritage Hotel," Michael noticed the letterhead. "That must be where he's staying. Shall I pop down? If You'll forgive my saying, because naturally it's Your decision, but I don't think it would be safe for You to leave."

"We're forgetting I could look from here. That's what he would have done so I'm sure I could do the same."

From his seat in Heaven, Gabriel thought about London and in an instant He'd found the hotel. Unfortunately, God's room was empty except for a cleaning woman changing the bed. She was muttering to herself, something about money and rich people trying to buy forgiveness.

"Sorry, it looks like he's gone. No clothes, nothing personal that I can see. Did he leave a forwarding address?"

"There's nothing on the message," Michael checked to make sure.

"Then We'll have to wait for his next call," Gabriel rubbed his eyes. "We'd better be prepared. I hope he's not angry. I blame Myself but he always made these things look simple."

Michael hoped Gabriel wasn't going to get Himself into a state. A crisis needed a calm Leader. Panic would help no one, least of all God somewhere down there in the chaos.

CHAPTER TWENTY

THE MAID HAD BEEN RIGHT, A LARGE PARTY HAD gathered near the entrance to the hotel and God was determined to make sure his reservation was secure. He needed reassurance and it was worth waiting to speak to his favourite receptionist one more time. There were others who wanted her attention too. It couldn't be easy being so slight and small and having everybody gravitate to her as soon as there was a crisis.

He chose a seat at the far side of the foyer so he could keep a lookout and be unobtrusive. The room was filled with activity but the chairs were comfortable and he drifted off in the perfumed atmosphere, unaware as Gabriel's presence swept through the lobby. The least sign would have alerted Heaven and cut short the traveller's sojourn on Earth. However, solutions and a way out weren't on God's mind as he opened an eye and glanced around. In fact, he wasn't thinking about anything at all except that he would have to get going pretty soon. Today could slip into tomorrow. Before he knew what was happening, it would be the next week and he would be extending his reservation for a second time.

God turned towards the desk. The receptionist was free, chatting to colleagues now that the new arrivals had been processed. He crossed the floor purposefully.

"Hello, Mr Godfrey, everything okay now?" she smiled. She had a soft spot for this quiet gentleman.

"Thanks to you." No flattery was intended. God truly did admire her manner and control. "I wanted to make sure my registration was in order. The cleaning lady told me the hotel was filling up and I saw so many new arrivals."

"No problem, let's have a look."

She tapped on the computer, fingers dancing across the keys. In a more elegant age, she would have been in the drawing room of a fine house, playing a piano with the same finesse.

"Yes, it's all fine. We have you booked in for another two weeks. Technically it's a new reservation so, if you don't mind, we could settle the account for the past few days and start afresh. Do you have your credit card with you? If not, we can do it later."

How could he refuse her anything? It was worth paying to be in the presence of someone competent and he gladly handed over the card. His well-practised signature satisfied every requirement. Not that she checked. That would have been disrespectful. G. Godfrey.

"Oh! In case you didn't realise, you'll have to speak to your bank, your card's nearly at its expiry date... Mr Godfrey, are you all right?"

God fell back. It was happening again. First they sent him out of Heaven, then they took his power and now they were taking his self-respect. He tried to pull himself together.

"Please... I... I don't know."

He was shaking and she was kneeling at his side with an arm around his shoulders. This wasn't the time for those petty rules telling you what you could and couldn't do. Mr Godfrey needed human contact.

He was looking better.

"I'm sorry, my dear, I don't know what came over me."

"I'll call a doctor. We'd better make sure there's nothing wrong."

"No, no," he protested, "I'll be all right in a moment. What were we talking about?"

"I was saying that you should contact your credit company. Your card is going to expire." Evidently he wasn't following. He must be unwell. She indicated to her assistant to get help.

"I don't understand, I've never had trouble like this before. How can you tell?"

Poor chap, she was thinking, he must have forgotten and was trying to cover up.

"You see this number down here? It shows the expiry date. 06 means June, so your card is valid for only one more month." She helped him to his feet and guided him to a seat across the foyer.

God breathed a sigh of relief. A month sounded like a reprieve. He smiled and took a deep breath before deciding not to recover too quickly. He enjoyed having this wonderful person all to himself.

"What do I do then?" he asked.

"Usually they send another in the post. If you're going to stay longer, you might want to get the replacement sent to us instead of to your home address."

"Thank you. Yes, I see. Do I phone them?"

"I think so. But let's not worry about that, you'll be going home before there's any problem. How are you feeling now?"

"Actually, my dear, I'm much better than I've been in days. I can't thank you enough." His confidence was restored, this must be the sign he had been waiting for.

A few weeks, a month at the most and he would be at home. What a relief.

"Do you want to see the doctor? His surgery is on Harley Street which is around the corner. I can call a cab if you like. Or we could ask him to come here."

"I don't think so. I feel fine. I'm sorry to have caused so much trouble."

Mr Godfrey was recovering but she was still worried.

"I'll get you a cup of tea. It won't take long. Oh, excuse me, they're calling me at the desk."

God settled into his chair. Five minutes of rest and relaxation would do no harm and, in any case, he still had to decide what to do next. This girl, young woman, should be promoted. He wouldn't have been left in limbo if she were in charge of Heaven. Anyway, it was clear that Gabriel and Michael could do with assistance. It would put their noses out of joint but she was destined for the top.

His reverie was interrupted by the arrival of the tea and a tray of sandwiches.

"Goodness gracious, who would ever have thought of meeting such an important person in the lobby of this hotel? Not I for one. Such a pleasure to see you."

God looked up. A motorcycle courier, top to toe

in black leathers, helmet in hand, was standing before his chair.

"Good morning," God said. This was turning into a very strange day. "I don't believe we've been introduced. My name is Godfrey."

"Ha ha. Very good, but I know who you are. Travelling *incognito*? Fact finding, I'm sure. You were always keen on knowledge."

Recognition at last, God tried to mask his relief, but from a quarter he could never have expected.

"Please, do not worry, your grand eminence. I'm not going to say anything," the motorcyclist chuckled.

"Thank you," God struggled to his feet. "If you could remind me…?"

The courier pulled off his sunglasses. His hair was tied back in a ponytail. There was something familiar about his face, and a definite twinkle in his eye.

God racked his memory for clues about this strange individual but nothing surfaced. Time was when these things would have been at his fingertips. Now they were buried somewhere in the past.

"I'm sorry, I can't place you."

The striking young man laughed. God snapped his fingers, relief and excitement colliding in mid-thought.

"Confu…!"

"Shh, shh. No names, if you don't mind. You never were discreet, always shouting and doing dramatic things. You should learn to be more quiet." But he shook God's hand enthusiastically. The foyer was buzzing with activity and the young man turned away with a conspiratorial wink. "I must go. It is time to fulfil my duty."

"Everything okay, Mr Godfrey?" the receptionist had come back. He could protest that he was improving but she wanted to be sure. "The doctor said he could be here in fifteen minutes if you want to see him."

"I've just met a friend," God couldn't help smiling. The youthful form of Confucius was handing over a package at the concierge's desk. God thought about waving but decided to practise discretion. "I'm feeling so much better. Thank you, my dear. I think I'll be fine."

"Okay, Mr Godfrey, if you're sure. Let me know if you change your mind."

"If you have time, I could do with some advice." God was feeling buoyant after two signs in quick succession.

"Of course," she was pleased the crisis had passed. She took a seat beside her guest, ready to help in any way she could. It was busy but Mr Godfrey had her attention.

"There are two things, really. First of all, I'm sorry about this morning," he began.

"You can't help it if you feel ill, Mr Godfrey."

"I meant when I locked myself out of the room."

"Oh, that. Don't worry, these things happen all the time."

"I thought I might have offended the maid." Now that he had made the decision to confess he was determined to continue. "I believe she thought I suspected her of interfering so I left a note and a little gift. I didn't know if that was the right thing to do. I don't want to cause offence."

"There's no need to worry, Mr Godfrey. I'll have a chat with Maria later and let her know how you feel. I'm sure she understood you were worried."

If it had been anybody else, God wouldn't have been confident the full import of his words was getting through but in her hands he felt safe.

"I'd like to speak to a lawyer and if you really think it's necessary I'll make an appointment to see your doctor. There are a few points to clear up because I want to get home as soon as possible."

"No problem at all," she said. "I have the details at the desk. As I mentioned, the doctor is on Harley Street and the lawyer... let me think. We've used a practice near Marylebone High Street in the past. I'm sure they'd be happy to see you."

"Thank you, it would be nice to walk if it's not too far. There are other things I need to do," God sat back to wait.

God was on autopilot as he walked away from the hotel remembering his previous life in rosy terms and confidently expecting a resumption of normal service. At last he was dealing with his problems and knew that he needed to carry cash in case the credit card expired before he was recalled home. Without money, he would end up needing to find employment to tide himself over. He stopped on the pavement thinking about Confucius working as a courier. He was delighted to have seen an old friend and knew he shouldn't have been surprised to find the sage happy with a lowly job. The mystics had always had peculiar ways, swapping from body to body to keep going. Confucius was a great mind and the architect of one of the most impressive of the earthly systems but God saw life differently. He couldn't help missing the privileges of his former status, and he still had plans for Heaven.

The first task of the day would be a visit to the bank. God lost himself in the pleasures of performing a substantial mission and was quietly satisfied to find the clerk accommodating when he showed his card and asked to make a cash withdrawal. The request was referred to the senior teller, a serious and unsmiling gentleman, but no surprise was expressed even at the magnitude of the suggested sum. God was informed that there was a trend away from hard currency in the world of electronic payments but, technicalities notwithstanding, these situations were not beyond the realms of their experience.

The bespectacled teller introduced the manager who took responsibility for money laundering regulations and assured the client that his account was in good order. The single obstacle, he explained, was the limited stock of banknotes held locally on the premises. A delivery from the central repository would need to be arranged once head office had authorised the release of funds. The full sum should be available from noon on the subsequent day although a proportion could be taken immediately.

"No problem," God said, enjoying the sound of his new motto. Tomorrow was well within the card's expiry period and life was under control. For a brief moment, he managed to forget Gabriel.

What next, he thought? The doctor or the lawyer?

151

He was inclined to be sceptical about these radical groups and, as far as he could remember, no lawyer occupied a senior position in Heaven. Nevertheless, people in this world believed in the system so there should be an outlet and representatives among the angels. At the very least, he should have a will in case he was recalled at short notice. He could leave his possessions to the girl at the hotel or even to the taxi driver, except that he didn't know her name.

The prospect of a consultation with a doctor was more confusing. He could have taken the opportunity to be seen at the hotel when he had felt ill but the indignity of being examined in public would have been impossible to overcome. And then there was the complication that Heaven was filled with medical errors, which suggested... if God wanted to get back to Heaven, should he go to a competent or an incompetent physician? It was a ridiculous situation. For that matter, he couldn't see how speaking to a lawyer could help either. If the receptionist had made the appointment, he would probably have to go.

CHAPTER TWENTY ONE

THERE WERE A NUMBER OF PITFALLS AWAITING GOD as he stepped brightly along the pavement. Workers lined the road, not so much digging as watching while one of their number drove a machine backwards and forwards creating havoc with the traffic. As before, near Primrose Hill, the workmen showed little interest in the mess. It was well known that the mayor's office had promoted a strategic plan to encourage people out of their cars but God couldn't help feeling irritated.

They'd never get away with this behaviour if he were in charge. And he couldn't understand why women attracted so many comments from the watching troupe even if it was clear a few *'ello darlin'*s didn't do much harm. Already, he was losing interest. He made sure the briefcase with his cash was secure. Now that he had decided against doctors and lawyers, he had nothing to do until he went back the next day to collect the remainder of the money from the bank. With no tasks left to perform he was starting to feel despondent. Unoccupied time could lead to thoughts, thoughts could lead to Heaven and to questions about why Gabriel had abandoned him. It was certainly suspicious. He would have done better if the shoe had been on the other foot.

He had forgotten the daily grind of existence before the start of his journey when he had been desperate to find a route away from drudgery and boredom. In London his mind could have been filled with signs and wonders but instead his thoughts were occupied with retribution, revenge and resentment that he had been trapped in a polluted city filled with louts and posturing pedestrians. This city was not a suitable place for a holiday and he was tired of pretending that everything was acceptable. The world needed a complete overhaul.

The heat of the day was intense. It was a while since the snack at the hotel and it had been easy to persuade himself that the fainting attack had been caused by anxiety about the credit card. His head was spinning and he felt unwell. His hand reached out for support, closed on thin air. Amid the hubbub of voices, he struggled to stay upright, lost his footing…

CHAPTER TWENTY TWO

...EVERYTHING WAS QUIET. ONLOOKERS WERE PAYING attention as they should have done before and God observed with satisfaction that the yellow machine had stopped. A throng of young men rushed along the pavement, hopefully they were friendly. It didn't matter, he was finally returning home. This would be the first time he would see Peter's reception centre from the other side.

The room was filled with people waiting to make their grand entrance to Heaven and the atmosphere of excitement was unmistakeable. God forced his way to the front of the crowd. Nobody would object as he took his rightful place.

"Hey you! There's a queue."

Heads turned to look at him. They wouldn't have much success with their applications if they didn't behave. If they weren't careful, God thought, they'd find out just how hard life could be.

He pushed on, ignoring as much as possible the barbed comments flying his way. The desk, directly ahead, was his goal. He'd be home and dry once he had passed through Peter's gate. Then he could come back to deal with this lot.

It wasn't Peter on duty. God didn't recognise the angel in charge, doubtless a new recruit. He arrived at the head of the line smiling with relief. Finally, he could relax. A few steps more and the ordeal would be over.

In accordance with established tradition, before he could pass through the barrier, God found himself reliving memories of life on Earth. Starting with arrival at Heathrow, those clothes and the mistake about the Elizabethan Age. The queues at the airport, the train, the taxi ride, meeting the taxi driver again and the disappointment to hear that she had a partner. How much he had enjoyed chatting, the invitation to have dinner when her son had appeared on the scene. Pride had played a…

"Okay, that's enough. There'll be plenty of time to dream about your lady friend when we're done."

God was startled into awareness. He had lost himself in thought. Everything about her was clear while other experiences paled into insignificance. Why was it that he had discovered what was important only when it was too late?

"I saw you pushing your way to the front. You won't find that kind of behaviour does you any favours. You won't fit in if you can't behave."

God was flabbergasted. No words came as the ignominy of the situation settled on him. This angel seemed an unlikely guardian of the entryway to Heaven.

"What's your name?" the official didn't bother trying to disguise impatience. "Don't make things difficult, my fine fellow. You can see how many people are waiting."

God was more than irritated. He'd been through a traumatic journey and he was not going to put up with insolence.

"God," he said.

"Yes, yes. You'll see him later if you get in," the angel leaned forward and spoke condescendingly. "But you'll have to tell me your name if you want to see the old chap, otherwise you can go to the back of the queue and wait until I've dealt with everyone else."

"I am God," the prospective entrant said loudly and clearly so there could be no mistake.

For a moment there was no reaction, then the crowd behind God's back tittered and there were comments.

"Look behind you. Do you see how many candidates are waiting?" the long-haired gatekeeper

157

looked down at the new arrival. They had arranged the desk to reflect the proper power relations. "This morning we've already had two Napoleons and an Elvis. I'm too busy for delusions. Now, tell me what name you were using on Earth."

God didn't like the way things were going but he had no choice.

"Godfrey. Mr Godwin Godfrey."

The angel looked up thinking that he had misheard a few moments before and been unnecessarily unpleasant. He glanced at the handwritten list. There was no printout or computer screen. God was surprised how backward things were up here. London was much more at the cutting edge.

"Sorry, old man. I don't have your name. Do you have any papers or permits?"

"No," God was losing hope. "Could you check? Please. I'm sure if you speak to Gabriel He'll confirm my position."

"I'm sorry, Godfrey," the keeper managed to summon a trace of sympathy, perhaps responding to the interviewee's patent desperation. "We get the list from Central Admissions at the start of the day and you come in only if we've had official notification, otherwise you go back down and try another time. I wouldn't be in such a hurry if I were you. Heaven's no piece of cake. You'll probably be happier going back to your old life."

"Couldn't you telephone Michael?"

The angel smiled, a toothy, joyless shark. Telephones, like all technologies that could have made their lives easier, had been banned by the almighty deity in a famous fit of pique.

"Oh yes, sure. I'd love to pick up the phone and call one of my buddies, Gabriel, Michael or even Jacob. Do you think if I had contacts like those I'd still be sitting here? I don't think so. Off you go, better luck next time," he dismissed the agitated form with a wave. "Oh please, don't be so ridiculous. Think about your lady friend and you'll be fine. Have a nice life, Godfrey. I did before I landed in this miserable place."

God made his way dejectedly from the desk. Most people were standing and crowding forwards. They had been promised redemption for so long and they weren't going to wait any longer than necessary. He couldn't really blame them, having done the same thing himself. He looked back to the gatekeeper who was sharing a joke with the next applicant in line. In his present circumstances God could see no alternative but to wait for the end of the angel's shift and hope for a more sympathetic reception next time around. He took a seat in the back row. Eventually Peter himself should make an appearance.

Suddenly he realised that the appearance of an advisor could distract from the quality of the advice. *Think about your lady friend*, the angel had said. As clear a reminder as God could hope for of everything he had left behind. And if he wanted to see his taxi driver again why was he knocking on Heaven's door? The revelation hit him like a blow on the chest. **Thud !**

What would be waiting if he managed to get through the barrier? More drudgery. Even in his dejected state, he had no trouble remembering the disheartening days, the endless routine of enquiries and trivial complaints. People didn't know how good they had it.

He looked around carefully, seized by a fear that he would be recognised. If Heaven didn't have him on their list all he had to do was stop praying and he could withdraw from view. This could be his last opportunity for freedom.

No-one appeared to have noticed the important change taking place. His heart was hammering as he tiptoed to the exit and chose the door marked

EARLY RETURNS — EARTH

"O G-o-d!"

The admitting angel's singsong voice called the one-time claimant to a halt. God's chest was tight, if only he had been more decisive. He turned around to face the music.

"Ha ha. Have a nice life, your holiness. They need someone like you down there. It's a lawless place."

The joke wasn't funny. The angel would be stuck behind a desk while Godfrey lived life to the full. He kept his mouth shut and pushed through the door. It was a long way down but nothing would hold him back. This time, he was looking forward to every moment.

AN INDEPENDENT LIFE

CHAPTER TWENTY THREE

Thud!

God opened his eyes. Someone was pushing on his chest and a man with a bushy moustache was trying to kiss him. He struggled, thinking he must have taken the wrong door. Using his arms and legs, he shoved as hard as he could. The man fell backwards and then sat watching as God tried to sit up, waiting for the chance to strike again.

There was so much noise. All around, road workers were clapping and chanting something that sounded like *Geezer*. The assailant waved to the crowd and God wondered if he could get away while the big man was distracted. This couldn't be London. If not Hell, it must be a less civilised place.

He tried to move but restraining hands held him back leaving no alternative but to wait. He was still feeling groggy and suffering from pain in his chest where the brute had punched and pushed him. The taste on his lips... he remembered the hairy man's kiss and wiped his mouth to be rid of the residue of burger and beer. A siren could be heard getting closer. A passer-by must have called the police. From one side, a reassuring voice was telling him not to struggle. He heard the words but he couldn't relax, not when the hooligan was so close and could attack without warning.

After an extended pause he tried again. This time, someone helped him upright as he cleared his throat.

"Where am I?" he asked, voice hoarse after the ordeal.

"Margaret Street," his supporter said. "You collapsed."

The memory returned as if from a dream. The world spinning and receding below. Resurrection, he had thought, until he had arrived in Peter's waiting room and realised that salvation was a step in the wrong direction.

"... and Geezer, over there, saved your life."

"Geezer? Saved me? That's ridiculous," God dismissed the suggestion. If he had stayed in the waiting room for even one more minute, the angel may have realised his mistake and there would have been no turning back. He tried to focus on his surroundings.

The Geezer was approaching and God steeled himself thinking the nightmare was going to start again. But the road-working foreman knelt at his side and spoke quietly.

"Are you all right now, sir? You gave us a fright, keeling over like that."

God nodded, still too traumatised to reason clearly.

"Hang on, if you can. The ambulance is on its way and you need to go to hospital to make sure it doesn't happen again."

Geezer stood up and looked around. The siren wasn't far off and he would be glad when professional help arrived. Resuscitation wasn't as easy as they made it look on the telly. The old man was battered and he hadn't said too much but that was hardly surprising. At least he was alive.

The ambulance crew pulled up and bustled about. The victim was delighted to be in official hands. Geezer didn't look much like a rescue worker. He was too big and dirty and the tattoos on his hands gave him away. 𝕾𝕬𝕿𝕬𝕹 and 𝕳𝕰𝕷𝕷 they said. The taste of onions lingered on.

With well-practised efficiency, the medics had God bundled up in no time. He was strapped onto a stretcher and a monitor was attached to record his heartbeat and vital signs. It was easy to be thorough in a pleasant part of London with sunshine on their backs. There were a few questions for God then they turned to interrogate the road worker. God wondered if they would take him into custody, or would police officers come in a separate vehicle? He felt dizzy with incomprehension as he watched the ambulance crew slapping the rough fellow on the back and offering congratulations. The world had gone completely mad. God didn't understand what these people were doing but he had no more strength to fight. To be kissed in the street was a most unpleasant experience. He squirmed and struggled against the restraints.

An alarm sounded and the ambulance men ran towards their patient.

"No," God shouted, "please don't hurt me."

Miraculously they stopped. A stray lead was re-attached and the heart monitor settled into silence.

"I don't think I can take any more of this. When I saw him lying there with his eyes closed and the monitor flatlined," Geezer said to the medics, clearly a little embarrassed. "Sorry, probably been watching too many movies. I'm sure you don't really talk like that."

"You did brilliantly so talk any way you like. We watch *Casualty* and *ER* too. Have you ever thought about joining the ambulance service?"

God, on the sidelines of the conversation, was finally catching on as the paramedics tried to persuade the Samaritan to give up road building. He could see that if no-one had taken the trouble to help, he would still be at the gates of Heaven waiting for Peter to show his face. He had a lot to thank this Geezer for. His life had been restored and he had been given a second chance. This time he could do something worthwhile.

It was important to be careful, that much was clear. Sooner or later Gabriel would come looking. It would be difficult to hide and God would need to be wary about what he said and did from now on. No more praying, that was important, and he should get away from the atmosphere of excitement as soon as possible. A near-death might attract the attention of precisely those he needed to avoid. He tried to loosen the straps that held him down.

"It's for your safety," the senior ambulance man said. "We don't want you falling out and injuring yourself." The words were offered kindly, with an attempt at humour to help God over the indignity of his captivity. "We'll release you as soon as we get to the hospital."

God made the decision not to protest. An emergency department was sure to be busy so it should be easy to get away.

"Setting off in a minute," the lead medic was in the cockpit, speaking quietly into his microphone. They loaded God into the back of the ambulance and the doors were closing when the passenger remembered his manners.

"I'm sorry to be a nuisance but there's something I need to do before we go."

"No problem," came the answer. His rescuers were delighted to be dealing with a coherent patient. Usually it was deaths, drunks, murders and mayhem.

"Do you think I could speak to that man?" God pointed towards Geezer. He knew the name but it was hardly a polite way to address someone who had saved him from a fate worse than death. Such an act deserved a decent display of gratitude.

The medic walked over to the workmen who were continuing with their extended break. A group had gathered around their new hero who blushed as he was led back to the ambulance.

"Thank you," God said. He wasn't sure what to do next. He couldn't explain the circumstances.

"Oh, don't worry. I'm sure you'd have done the same for me," Geezer said cautiously.

Was that true? God had ignored his saviour before

the incident. If a man like this had collapsed, God would have thought he was drunk and walked on by.

"No, no, you don't understand. I can't explain what this means to me."

Geezer didn't want to be offensive but he'd had enough. It was one thing doing mouth-to-mouth on some old fart but he wasn't a great one for talking. Road building and his JCB were a lot easier to handle than this lot. The ambulance crew came to his rescue and began making moves to take the patient to hospital. They couldn't justify hanging about any longer.

God put out his hand, once mighty and strong, now ordinary and a little shaky after his recent experience. Geezer took the opportunity and was surprised to find the patient had any strength left at all. God thought about promising to repay the favour but that was a practice from his distant past. He must get used to a different life. He must get used to being ordinary.

It was time to get away from the scene of the incident. God released his grip on Geezer who looked relieved as the doors closed. The ambulance manoeuvred about and pulled into the traffic with siren wailing even though it may have been preferable to be more discreet.

They stopped with a jerk and the driver hopped

out. God hoped nothing was wrong.

"Your new friend is looking after you again. Is this briefcase yours?" the paramedic asked.

God felt another thump in his chest but the tracing on the heart monitor showed no change. All his resources, everything, could so easily have been lost.

"Yes," he said weakly.

"Can you tell us what's here? We need to know so we can be sure it really belongs to you," the crew had opened the case and were looking at God's cache of banknotes.

"A credit card, money, a guidebook. My passport. You can check the photograph," God suggested anxiously. London wasn't cheap and it was going to be difficult getting started on his independent life.

"You'd better take it now. There will be a ton of paperwork if we arrive carrying a bag with so much cash."

After another noisy start, the siren was turned off although the lights were still flashing. It was as inconspicuous as an ambulance could be but they made quick progress through daytime traffic to the hospital. God was unloaded at A&E where an initial assessment was performed. He looked like a refugee wrapped in a blanket and clutching the briefcase like a talisman. The important thing was that he had survived. Stress or whatever had brought on the attack of dizziness had finally disappeared.

Once the ambulance crew had departed, God settled into a seat in the waiting area. A notice board next to the main desk indicated a delay of approximately four hours and nobody was in a rush to deal with a pedestrian and un-protesting patient. It was hardly comfortable and God didn't want treatment anyway. Finding the exit was easy compared to the route away from Heaven. The hospital staff were busy with emergencies and nobody was paying attention.

CHAPTER TWENTY FOUR

GOD STEPPED TENTATIVELY INTO THE STREET. HE FELT well enough but his self-belief was at a low ebb and he needed to eat. There was nothing in view except a public house called *The Jeremy Bentham*. His clothes were scruffy after the day's activities but probably acceptable in the modern age.

Avoiding the gathering of professional drinkers, he ordered at the bar before taking a seat in the indoor eating area. It was time to sit back and consider the situation carefully, certainly too early to savour freedom. He needed to tread carefully and plan his next move before making decisions.

Gabriel might not be looking yet but eventually someone would pick up the messages he had left over the weekend. And when they realised what had happened at Peter's gate there would be a crew trawling through London to contact him. There were two things to his advantage though. First, they'd be assuming he wanted to be found so they'd keep their search to areas he had visited before. The hotel would be the foremost place they'd look. Second, and maybe more important, Gabriel wouldn't want to risk panic if the story leaked out and that meant He would have to be discreet.

God sat quietly. The sunshine had drawn all other customers outside and nobody paid attention to the dishevelled gentleman hiding alone in the shadows with his briefcase concealed under the table for safety.

Money! he thought suddenly, that was sure to be a problem. They might not know he was carrying a credit card but they'd find out, and they would be able to trace every transaction. He had to get back to the bank before they realised what was happening. After that, he would need to reconsider.

There were other problems too, the most immediate of which was finding accommodation. He'd have to choose a new hotel and it would be sensible to move to a new area to throw them off the scent although a border crossing was out of the question. In any case, a country like England with its healthy distrust of authority had significant advantages.

He looked through the briefcase. Aside from the bank notes, there was his wallet, the passport, notepaper and the taxi driver's card. A sign? God breathed a sigh of relief before chastising himself for loose thinking. And it would be better to stop thinking of himself as God. It would have to be Godwin Godfrey from now on.

It was a small logical step but he realised that all his plans could collapse in an instant. If the bank knew the name he was using then Gabriel would too. He was going to have to start completely afresh. Very hard though to pick something at random. He looked around for inspiration but found himself wondering instead about the pub in which he was sitting.

"Excuse me, miss," God called across the room to the barmaid. His accent had changed subtly, sounding more London now that he had made the decision to stay.

She looked up.

"This Mr Bentham, is he the manager or the owner? I presume he lives on the premises and that's why we see his name."

From behind the bar, the girl looked at the customer blankly. She knew he couldn't be drunk. He'd only had a half of something but you never knew with these old men from the hospital. Probably drinking medicinal brandy before breakfast.

"Jeremy Bentham?" God pointed to the name of the pub.

"Oh," she said.

Surely, Godfrey thought, it was a reasonable question. Why was she having trouble with an answer?

"The manager's called Matt. He's from Australia." And that was all. She went back to polishing glasses.

It wasn't entirely what God had expected but if the name attracted so little interest it might be suitable for his new life. Jeremy Bentham was exactly who he would be. After the trials he had been through, at last he was making progress.

He finished his food and and made ready to leave, continually adding items to his mental checklist. Accommodation and money were at the top of the agenda but there were other things to consider like shoes, clothes and a new toothbrush. The world was filled with practicalities and endless complications.

Wandering down towards Oxford Street, God found himself outside a bookstore and surveyed the shelves from the pavement through oversized windows. He was no longer a tourist and a simple map was more appropriate than the guide book on which he had come to depend. He tossed the book into a litter bin, made his way into the shop and selected a substitute. When it came to paying, God was careful to do everything correctly. He caught himself in time. It can be tricky remembering who you are without the benefit of a familiar label. Jeremy Bentham wanted no trouble and the credit card carried too great a risk. He reminded himself to pay with cash.

As usual, there was a queue at the till and, being an ordinary man, Jeremy waited impatiently for his turn. The sales assistant scanned the little map and waited for the money. He offered a £50 note but she looked sceptical, behaving as if he had done something wrong.

"Is something the matter?" he asked, voice and accent slipping as he grew more anxious.

"You'll need to give me something smaller. The company doesn't accept large notes," she said.

Jeremy didn't know what to think. He was in the right. There had been no trace of an apology at the breakdown in service and he was determined not to give in to unreasonable behaviour. The salesperson, in contrast, had no qualms. She had been in London long enough to know it wasn't worth fighting the system whereas he was marked out as a newcomer expecting a symbolic moment. Fairness and justice must triumph.

She reached past him and served the next customer. Neither gave him a second glance, although the security guard was paying attention. The shop was calm and quiet but bookish types could be difficult and the guard adjusted his cap in preparation for the inevitable confrontation. It wasn't pleasant ejecting people from the store but this was the job he had signed up for and he would do his best even if his heart wasn't in the matter.

Jeremy caught the security officer's eye. The last thing he needed was trouble from an official and he decided it would be better to stick to the guidebook after all. He left the map on the counter and set about retrieving his book from the waste bin on the pavement.

From inside the shop, the guard watched the customer going through the rubbish and was pleased the incident had passed off without aggravation. The old man should have known not to make trouble, but then anybody capable of making sensible judgements probably wouldn't be in such a terrible state in the first place. He brought his attention back to the melee of customers and unending rows of shelves. It wasn't that he was unsympathetic but he was employed to protect the business. He'd offer up a prayer on Sunday.

Jeremy was oblivious as he looked around for a place to sit while he leafed through the newly recovered guide. London was a big place and he didn't want to waste time. He grimaced. The pages were now filthy and the map was useless. It showed only the centre of the city with notes about tourist attractions. He tossed the battered book away once more and resolved to eat humble pie. He would have to try again in the shop.

The security guard noticed as he entered and whispered into the little telephone on his shoulder. Soon there were two more of them, simply standing and watching for the time being. Jeremy knew he was outnumbered and beat a hasty retreat.

The guards dispersed and the store returned to normal. One disgruntled customer was an irritation but the course of the enterprise wouldn't be diverted. Except for a mental note made by a security guard about the unfortunates of the world, the bookshop reverted to its torpid state.

Jeremy knew he had to put distance between himself and the latest setback. With everything he had been through, the day was turning out to be very frustrating. It was the first day, he told himself, and things would be better in the morning.

Paved with gold? Hardly, he thought as he plodded along the pavement to find a place to stay somewhere near the bank. He could hear himself thinking aloud but what could he do? It was hard to break a long-standing habit.

CHAPTER TWENTY FIVE

GABRIEL WAS FEELING UNEASY. GOD MIGHT HAVE SAID that he wanted to be alone but as Leader of the team in Heaven, He could have kept a discreet eye on the situation. He knew Michael thought He was taking advantage of God's absence to lord it over His minions but it wasn't true. He'd give everything to put the clock back and have God in his rightful place. This job was no fun at all, and when One found Oneself summoning former associates it simply highlighted the inequality of the relationship. No wonder things were going wrong.

"Oh, hi there, Mike. How's everything?"

Michael was less than pleased. He had been busy but Gabriel had forgotten very quickly that there were things to be done. It was very disruptive being dragged back and forth for no good reason.

"Everything's in order, except for you-know-what." They had taken to speaking in code to minimise the risk of the great secret leaking out.

"Don't be angry, Mike, I can't control this thing. I

was only thinking about you. I'm not trying to make things difficult. Honestly."

Michael softened a little. He could understand that he had to come when he was summoned by Gabriel's thoughts so why didn't Gabriel think about God? That would bring the old man back and then the trouble would be over. He and Gabriel could go back to their usual roles. It was impossible to behave normally while Heaven was in this strange position.

"I would like to, you know," Gabriel said.

"I'm sorry, You would like what?"

"I want to think about bringing God back but I can't do it. He gave very strict instructions. Believe Me, I'd be very pleased to see him."

Michael had forgotten that his thoughts would be available to Gabriel. There was no hiding anything and that was the root of the problem. He knew everything about you but you couldn't know about Him. Not unless He chose to speak.

"Exactly," Gabriel agreed.

"How about…?"

"Go on, it's a good idea," Gabriel urged, leaning forward in His seat.

Michael struggled. The suggestion was only half-formed in his mind.

"Okay, I'm not sure of this so I hope it doesn't come out wrong," he wasn't sure if he had spoken but Gabriel nodded to show He understood. "There are two options to consider but, first of all, You really do have to make a formal decision about whether or not You want God back."

It was a risky position to take. It could be the end if Gabriel made the wrong choice. Michael waited.

"Yes, that's the point. I could easily take over, couldn't I? Rule the world, Gabriel, King of the Universe."

Michael found himself holding his breath.

"But I don't want that, do I? Otherwise We wouldn't be talking!" Gabriel was on His feet. "The whole point is that I want help. You have no idea the stress I'm under. It's so easy for the rest of you."

"Then we have to find him," Michael said with relief. The outburst didn't worry him. Gabriel needed to let off steam and there was nobody else around. It was clear that underneath the grandeur, the old Archangel was struggling to get out.

"But how, Mike? We've looked everywhere; he must be hiding. Is that what you're saying?" Gabriel was being careful to include the junior partner in the decision-making. It was unnecessary but Michael appreciated the gesture and played his part. It was better for the two of them to be working as a team.

Gabriel was pleased to have resolved the issue. He sat back and prepared to tell Michael everything.

"Nothing I try does any good. I've been wondering about London, thinking that anybody might fall ill or collapse somewhere in the street. So many things could have gone wrong so I checked the hotel again, and every church listed in that file of messages. Surely he would have stayed in the same place if he wanted Us to contact him? There was no trace but I had the strangest feeling he was close today. It felt like I could have reached out and touched him, only I didn't know where to reach."

Their old leader would have known what to do and without him they were at sea even if the power had stayed in Heaven.

"I don't see that there's anything more I can do." Gabriel ground to a halt at the sound of someone hammering on the door.

The two senior figures adjusted their posture so that a suitable air of formality pervaded God's antechamber where they were meeting to preserve the illusion of normality. It was important not to give any sign there was a crisis.

"Come," said Gabriel, playing His part to perfection. The strain wasn't showing at all.

Peter came through the door, dragging a lesser angel by the ear.

"I need to see God," he said.

Michael's heart sank but Gabriel easily met the challenge.

"You know I can't disturb him when he's involved in this new project. We have to wait until he gives Us a sign."

Michael was filled with admiration. It was all true, Gabriel was unmistakeably in command.

"I can't wait. What am I going to do with this lout?" Peter gestured towards the scowling figure hovering near the door.

"Michael and I have time, why don't you tell Us? We'll let God know as soon as he's ready. Oh, come on, Peter. Sit down, relax, you're far too tense. What's got you so upset?"

No choice was offered. There might have been things to do but Gabriel was imperious and nobody felt able to protest. *Where to begin?* Peter gathered his thoughts.

"The beginning would be best," Gabriel said.

Michael was surprised. He wasn't privy to anyone's

contemplations but he worried that Gabriel had missed a trick.

"Oh sorry, I didn't realise I had spoken," Peter said, a little flustered. "I've talked to God about these problems before and this time we need to act."

"I'm not following. Tell Me everything," Gabriel made it clear He was interested.

"It's far too complicated to explain from the beginning. Probably better if I wait until God's free. I know he'll understand."

Play it cool, Michael thought, he knew Gabriel would get the message. Gabriel glanced over but gave no other sign.

"Okay, if you're sure there's nothing We can do to help."

"Honestly, I'm at my wit's end. This ruffian has been throwing people out of Heaven without proper authority. We never know where they'll end up if we send them back unprepared. It's a long way back to Earth without a guide and You know how Lucifer loves a falling angel."

"Sounds extraordinary. Something happened today, did it?" Gabriel asked to keep the conversation going. Eventually, He would get the story.

"I've had reports, and this time they're documented

187

because there were witnesses. Honestly, we're the gatekeepers and I don't like people getting a bad impression when they arrive," Peter paused for breath. It was clear he felt a deep responsibility and he cast a poisonous glance in the direction of his subordinate. "I've had a day, I can tell you. Calming newcomers and reassuring them."

"All right," said Gabriel, turning to the younger angel. "What's your name?"

"Geldof," came the sullen reply.

"Okay, angel Geldof, tell Us what you did. Let's hear your side of the sorry tale."

Both Peter and Michael were surprised. This wasn't how God would have handled the situation. God fancied himself as terrible and jealous but it didn't suit Gabriel. He was more of a conciliator.

"Come on, what is this?" Peter interjected irritably. "You don't need to speak to him."

"Let's hear what Geldof has to say, shall We?" Gabriel could do steel if it were needed and Peter was forced to resume his seat.

"This old man arrived. His name wasn't on the list but it didn't stop him pushing his way to the front and demanding special treatment," the angel looked across to see how the story was going down.

"Carry on."

"I was on duty by myself and it gets a bit crazy with all those people shoving. I couldn't help laughing when he demanded I call for help. You know what God said about telephones. Anyway, I told him the rules and he went."

"He went where?" Peter prompted.

"He went, that's all I know. It's not my job to watch over everybody."

"There's more, isn't there?" Peter insisted. "Tell Gabriel and Michael everything unless you want me to do it for you."

"Well," Geldof took a moment before continuing. "He had this funny name. I asked for his details so I could check on the list and he said *God*. We always get a few jokers and it got a laugh. It was good to release the tension."

There was a sharp intake of breath all around. Taking the Lord's name in vain wasn't acceptable even if it was becoming more common. That was Peter's interpretation. Gabriel and Michael lived in a rarefied atmosphere and they hadn't been exposed to the unfortunate trend. They, on the other hand, were thinking something entirely different.

"Then he told me his real name was Godwin

Godfrey. I guess God was a nickname or something but it made no difference – there was still nothing on the list so I sent him away," the lanky angel was smug, nobody was going to throw him out on this charge. He had stuck to procedures, or near enough. This was simply Peter having his periodic temper tantrum.

"That is quite enough," Gabriel cut in. He was not going to have some junior thinking of Peter in that way.

Everybody was shocked and a little awed. Michael hoped He hadn't gone too far.

"So, you sent this Godwin away," Gabriel said in a tone that mixed sweetness with authority. "Where did he go?"

"I already said I don't know. He was going through the door when I last saw him. He looked determined and he definitely wasn't upset. Not like…" Geldof gestured towards his manager.

"Yes, yes. Let's stick to the point," Peter interrupted. "You can see why I need to speak to God."

Gabriel and Michael needed to consult. They needed to know where God or Godwin, whatever he was called, had got to. They should be able to contact him if he had made it back to Earth.

There was no time for hand wringing. Action was required.

"Angel Geldof, what else do you have to say?"

"Me? Nothing. Only that he was delighted to be getting back to his lady friend."

Michael looked across at Gabriel who shrugged. Maybe they had the wrong person after all. Assistance was summoned and they waited while the recidivist junior was taken away.

"Peter, Michael, this is what we're going to do," Gabriel had made a decision. "We need to know everything about this Godwin character. Where he came from, where he went after your trainee sent him down. We're going to find him and We're going to offer him another chance."

"And Geldof?"

"Confined to quarters. Nobody is to see him or speak to him. I'm sure God will be delighted to deal with this matter in due course," Gabriel rose from his chair. "I know it's late but I don't think We can let this wait until tomorrow."

Peter's first instinct was to protest at the severity of the response but he thought better of it. He had come asking for action and his wish had been granted even if some aspects of the situation were mystifying.

"Yes, of course, I'll put someone on it right away. I hope poor Mr Godfrey hasn't been taken."

"Me too," Gabriel gave a wan smile. Michael said nothing, there was no need for him to speak.

As the door closed behind Peter, Gabriel slumped down in His chair.

"What do you think?"

"I think it's God," Michael said out loud to be sure the thought was clear.

"So do I," Gabriel agreed. "And I wouldn't be surprised if Lucifer has taken him. There's something about that Geldof. Do you think he's working for the other side?"

"I doubt it. An assignment under Peter would drive me crazy too," Michael laughed. "Anyway, there's nothing to be done about them now so if You don't mind I'll go down and take a look at London myself."

"That's fine. If you can't find him, I'm going to have to tell Peter the whole story. There won't be any choice," Gabriel considered the options. "At least We have a proper excuse for looking now."

I don't see why You needed excuses in the first place, Michael bit his tongue.

"Leave that to Me to worry about," Gabriel responded sharply to the intrusive thought. "Your job is to check what happened on Earth. If he's there, this time it should be easy for you to bring him home."

Michael resolved to do his best.

"All right, off you go," Gabriel said wearily. "Let's hope this doesn't take too long. We'll meet first thing in the morning. By then, there should be news."

Things were moving on Earth and in Heaven, and the principals were destined for a sleepless night. In contrast, Geldof was relaxed. The more he thought about the whole situation, the better his position seemed to be. The lure of do-goodery without red tape had been irresistible but the reality of day-to-day life in an administrative backwater had turned out to be boring. Every one of his colleagues was obsessed with rituals and the pecking order and their days were filled with menial tasks, cross-checking lists and processing applicants. Professionally speaking he had been better off in his previous job, and his friends had been more exciting too. The tape might not be red in Heaven but the silver lining was just as constricting.

Things might work out after all. He hadn't planned it this way but if they sent him down it would be fine. It would be back to Earth, of course. He didn't imagine they would want him to go anywhere else. Tell the Truth, was the mantra taught to all new recruits and that's exactly what he had done. Heaven was a miserable place and he couldn't help it if harsh reality was too much for some aspirant angel. He would appeal if they gave him Hell. He'd appeal if he had to go all the way to God himself. It looked like win-win for Geldof as he settled down in his cell. In Heaven it was easy to get comfortable.

In more salubrious surroundings, Peter had no idea of the magnitude of the crisis and he entertained himself with the happy thought of swapping the lost Mr Godfrey for Geldof if things had gone wrong. Purgatory would suit that one perfectly, in Peter's opinion. Not that it counted for much with God in purdah and Gabriel acting as if He was in charge. Neither He nor Michael would consent to a prisoner exchange but it didn't stop Peter smiling as he imagined Geldof turning on a spit above a pool of molten magma. The only problem was that the scruffy angel would soon be outdoing his tormentors. Peter found his thoughts guided back to the matter at hand. The punishment issue would have to wait. Nothing could be done until they had been through the investigation.

Gabriel and Michael were contemplating more active interventions. Leaving Gabriel to fret, Michael calculated the time difference. It was late afternoon and not many hours since the fall. If Godwin Godfrey had managed to find his way back to London, it wouldn't take long to reach him. By common consent they refrained from discussing the worst-case scenario.

CHAPTER TWENTY SIX

THE TRAIL WAS STILL WARM AND MICHAEL FOLLOWED God from the reception centre at Peter's Gate to the street corner in central London where the resuscitation had taken place. There were barriers relating to excavations in the roadway but no police presence, a sign that led to the conclusion that the landing hadn't been too unpleasant. The details were noted. In due course Mr Geezer could expect his reward but for the present Michael was determined to pursue all leads as quickly as possible.

The ambulance was easy to track from reports and telephone calls logged at the control centre. Once inside the hospital, things became more difficult. The trail got cooler and suddenly went cold altogether. It was certainly awkward, not to say downright strange. God should have been in plain view by now and an A&E department was the perfect place to arrange a meeting and swift repatriation. The procedures were well established.

He checked again to see if anything would come

to light. The ambulance had arrived with Godwin and left empty to go on the next call. In the interim, the patient had been handed over to hospital staff where triage had taken place. Michael needed to know if the fugitive was still waiting for attention.

He adopted a disguise as a member of staff and made his way down the drab corridor to the waiting area where he found a collection of patients in various stages of life and decomposition. There was certainly nobody on the benches who vaguely resembled a deity and a notice on the wall suggested a waiting time of four hours. Unless they had miscalculated, the patient should have been seen ages ago.

Now that he knew God had returned to Earth, Michael was determined not to return to Heaven empty-handed. He was about to search through the cubicles inside the treatment area when the matron arrived to challenge his presence. Michael slipped smoothly into a persona he had used before.

"Good afternoon, I'm looking for Mr Godwin Godfrey who was brought in by ambulance five hours ago," nurse Michael said confidently, looking at the watch on his lapel,

"And you are?" The matron's eyes narrowed, nothing escaped her scrutiny. She had never laid eyes on this handsome senior nurse and he would have to pass inspection before information could be handed out.

"I'm from the Post-Resuscitation Task Force. We're a research team affiliated to the MRC," Michael explained his interest in patients with a particular profile. "Notification has been submitted that Mr Godfrey was rescued by a member of the public and we're arranging follow-up."

The matron agreed to help. Any member of her profession deserved attention even if they insisted on doing spurious surveys. She looked through the admission cards of patients still waiting to be seen. If Mr Godfrey had been resuscitated, the triage system would have ensured he was dealt with as soon as possible, after the backlog of actually dying patients had been cleared.

The notes were waiting in the pile. Godwin Godfrey had been accepted in the department, seen by a nurse – the matron noted the time stamp – he should have been dealt with hours ago. It was a striking delay which would stand out in the monthly audit. With Michael in tow, she made a thorough search of the waiting area, waking every drunk and questioning each prospective patient. If Mr Godfrey had collapsed once it could easily happen again. The hospital had an excellent reputation and she didn't want him dying quietly in some corner. The place for dying was in the high-dependency unit, surrounded by trained staff.

As they were walking, Michael examined the file of documents. The signature from the ambulance man was illegible but that was hardly relevant.

"Do you think we could speak to the triage person? That might help."

"Yes, we had better do that," the matron led the way forward. "If something goes wrong, this could turn into a major incident."

The student nurse was soon located but had little to add. The initial consultation had been routine. It was what happened afterwards that was worrying, and of that there was no record. Maybe the record was accurate, Michael realised. It was possible that nothing had actually happened.

"Would you mind if I asked some questions?" he asked politely.

"Of course. You go ahead," the matron replied for her younger colleague. "I'll have a word with security."

Michael turned to the nurse. Her hair was neatly pulled back and she wore discreet makeup with an air of competence that couldn't be denied. He gave a quick glance at her name badge and noted the details on his clipboard.

"This won't take long, Elizabeth. Tell me everything you remember. Is there anything more than is written in the notes?" he asked. She was too young to be surrounded by pain and suffering but didn't seem to mind.

"Not really," she thought carefully. "He looked okay or, at least, he didn't complain of anything. His clothes were rumpled but you would expect that if he collapsed in the street. There was a briefcase, I think."

She smiled at Michael who nodded for her to continue.

"Mr Godfrey was happy, free, like he had escaped from something awful. I suppose it must have been to do with having a near-death experience."

Michael had stopped paying attention. The nurse was a pleasant girl who took her job seriously but there was nothing useful in these recollections.

"Will you be needing me for anything else?" she asked.

"No, thank you,' Michael forced his thoughts back to the matter at hand. "You've been most helpful. Let's hope Mr Godfrey's okay."

"Oh, I'm sure he's all right. He looked fine when I saw him leave."

"I beg your pardon?"

"Mr Godfrey left hours ago," she offered tentatively.

"Why didn't you say so before?"

"I didn't know." Tears were brimming in her eyes. Nurse Michael was becoming so fierce he was in danger of losing his disguise. "You didn't say anything about that, you asked about triage. I thought you were doing my assessment."

Michael stood back. Earth was turning out to be more complicated than he remembered. It was true, he hadn't chosen the right questions.

"Do you know where he went?" he tried again, sounding as kind as he could manage.

"I saw him walking out unaccompanied so I thought he had been discharged," a hesitant smile returned to her face. "I was on a coffee break. He went down Huntley Street, that way, towards the pub on the corner."

"All right, young lady. You are going to make a statement right now." The matron had returned from her enquiries empty-handed. "If Mr Godfrey left without informing us, it is not our fault. If he discharges himself and then gets into trouble, there is no way it can be construed as our responsibility."

"I'm sorry, I didn't know you were searching for him," the nurse looked back as she was led away but Michael was no longer listening. Without bothering to change, he went directly to the pub.

Jeremy Bentham? Michael had a sinking feeling as he looked in from the doorway. The unseasonable warmth from earlier in the day had been overtaken by familiar English rain and the rooms inside were filled to bursting. Michael couldn't imagine God choosing a place like this. Anyway, he reminded himself, the nurse had only said that he walked towards the pub. She didn't actually see him going inside. Michael turned to go. The only thing he had learnt was that God had made it safely down to Earth. There was no need for Gabriel to say anything more to Peter.

CHAPTER TWENTY SEVEN

TAKE REFUGE IN ACTION, JEREMY THOUGHT. IT WAS no good standing on the street corner thinking of what might have been. This was the time for decisions and first among them must be finding somewhere to stay. Unfortunately, he discovered when he raised his eyes from the pavement, instinct had brought him directly back to the Heritage Hotel on Portland Place.

He looked wistfully up towards his old room and found himself hankering after the comfortable life, free of the overwhelming sense of insecurity that accompanied every action. However, he had chosen the path of a fugitive and something less grand was now appropriate. There were many choices and no reason to be worried.

Be that as it may, life was determined to present obstacles. From Marylebone through Mayfair to Hyde Park, every place he tried turned out to be full. The receptionists were polite and some had advice but opportunities in the West End were limited. He was going to have to try farther afield.

Beggars can't be choosers, he reminded himself. It was an expression he had heard so many times. Following directions from a friendly doorman, he set off on foot for the fertile fields of Bloomsbury, looking for a place called Clerk and Well.

The route along Oxford Street was as busy as usual and, looking down at his dusty jacket, he realised that the time had come to buy new clothes. After only a few minutes, he found himself in a menswear shop with a sales assistant who was much the same as the young man who had given him advice over his first breakfast so many days ago. It was an outdoor activity kind of place. Jeremy noted the profusion of shirts and fleeces and explained what he needed.

"Clothes and shoes. And I'll need a suitcase," he said after only a moment's hesitation.

"No problem. Let's get started," the youth examined the middle-aged form standing before him and began guiding his customer towards the pleasures of a contemporary life. "Better if we avoid the trendy stuff, I think. Are you going on holiday?"

There was no reason for the salesman to make a personal enquiry and Jeremy was immediately suspicious. He took the opportunity to lay a false trail.

"I'm setting off for Russia next week. Hill walking and geographical exploration," he answered carefully. Catching him wasn't going to be easy.

"I've never been anywhere like that," the lad was undoubtedly impressed. "I suppose it will be hot at this time of the year. You won't be needing thermals."

More complications. Jeremy paused for thought. Either he had to persist with the story or be caught out. "I'll need everything except a tent. I have one already."

"No problem," the salesman said. Again.

The response was starting to grate. How could everything be *no problem* when the world was plagued by difficulties. And now he had started telling lies.

Nevertheless, and despite his qualms, the business of buying clothes proceeded effortlessly. Jeremy had imagined measurements and tailoring but such complexity belonged to a different age. Modern fabrics and standardised sizes proved to be handy and trouble free. In no time an impressive pile of purchases had gathered at the till.

"Could I ask your advice...?" Jeremy began, but broke off when he remembered that trouble could arise without warning. And questions, like answers, could give away information best kept to himself.

"No problem."

Were these words the limit of the boy's vocabulary? He had to restrain himself from overt criticism. He gathered his possessions, there was no reason to prolong the agony.

"Thank you for your help."

Jeremy stepped back onto Oxford Street, feeling more assured. The visit to the shop had provided more than the simple transaction he had anticipated. Uncertainty had been displaced by a resurgence of old ambitions, and it had become clear that some of the changes made under a cloud of dejection and despondency would have to be undone. Chief among the errors was the adoption of a spurious name.

He might be labouring under difficult circumstances, he may need a label if he was challenged, but there was no need to fool himself – God he was and God he would be. Gabriel may have been left with the power, but the spirit was on Earth. He walked taller on the pavement. For too long he had been struggling with trivialities and the mundane and on the streets of Bloomsbury God rediscovered himself. Once again he could look forward to being the one who could separate darkness and dispense with chaos. Let those juniors try to catch him, they would get a run for their money.

The twists and turns of life felt like one of the rollercoasters he'd seen in advertisments for a holiday theme park. He had no final destination in mind but there was no trace of indecision as he made his way eastwards to put distance between himself and the old haunts. Illness, delays on a train or losing contact with colleagues in Heaven might once have been significant but God realised that he was starting to enjoy himself. He felt in control and close to omnipotent as he marched along. The journey had become bearable and he made good progress, soon finding his way to Holborn.

In keeping with his new world view, he wanted to be with the smart business set and avoid tourists, even if he had to pay for the privilege. Spend your way out of a depression, he thought, or should that be recession? He was unemployed for the moment but the bank was holding his money and he could afford a bed in keeping with his status. Soon after crossing Kingsway, he noticed a hotel without the pretence of olde England that had characterised his last home.

His clothes marked him out as a modern entrepreneur rather than an unfashionable businessman but no-one commented. There were indeed rooms available and the receptionist, an elegant man with an air of stylish modernity, was ready to make the arrangements. He logged into the hotel booking system and offered his guest a suite.

"That won't be necessary," God said firmly. "I'm only here overnight."

"Very good, sir. If I could ask you to complete our registration form? And then I'll need your credit card."

God was thinking on his feet and the first test was easily passed.

"Unfortunately my documents were stolen this morning," he said, feeling strong enough to tempt fate. "I can't give you a card but I am happy to pay in advance or leave a cash deposit if that will help."

The mood of confidence prevailed. Self-assurance was patently a prerequisite for success. As he was counting out notes from the wallet in his briefcase he realised he would need somewhere to stay after the visit to the bank the next day. Without wavering, he took the precaution of paying for an extra night.

The room was pleasant and quiet. A large bed, TV, minibar; the usual, tasteful stuff. God wandered around, admiring the practicality of the arrangements. He should have trusted himself to find somewhere suitable. Despite a resolution to remember, it was difficult to recreate desperate feelings now that he was well-dressed and settling into a new home. There wasn't much else to do. The old suit needed to be cleaned but the laundry could deal with that in the morning.

The old choices presented themselves while he was unpacking. Eat in or eat out? Restaurant or room service? God sat on the edge of the bed as a wave of weariness replaced the excitement of recent exploits. Room service, he concluded. He was too tired to change and there would be adventures enough in the morning. In any case, tea and a sandwich were exactly what he needed.

Sound from the television drifted across the room and God looked up as the face of a familiar newscaster appeared on-screen. If Gabriel had started looking, there would have been some sign of disruption but the headlines were unremarkable and bland which must mean that he was safe. Even the weather pattern was holding.

"The balmiest spring since records began," he heard the forecaster say.

God glossed over the significance of the news team's excitement at a less-than-significant weather update. His thoughts had moved on to the tasks of the morning as he waited for his food to arrive.

TRIALS OF IMMIGRATION

CHAPTER TWENTY EIGHT

MORNING HAD BROKEN AND IT WAS LIKE THE FIRST
morning. God awoke in an unfamiliar bed with a
disorientation that took time to clear. He changed,
patted his pockets to make sure he had the key to his
room and set off.

A tendency to dress down was evident in the
business community and he looked suitably informal
as he chose a quiet spot to have breakfast, to gather his
thoughts and prepare for the day. He gave his order
with no need for conversation or advice. His plans
were clear and he flicked idly through the newspapers
while he waited to get started.

As usual, the financial pages took longest. The
calculations looked impressive but what was the point
of mathematical rigour for something as intrinsically
inaccurate as economics? Most of the reporting was
simple gossip with a seasoning of analysis tossed in.
All things considered, he preferred the tabloids. Times,
Guardian, the Mirror. They were easier to handle,
with pictures and comfortably large type. Curious

how things work out. You could make plans but once your creations were let loose they had minds of their own. He paged through The Sun, finding nothing of particular interest until a familiar face caught his eye. Mr Geezer was in the paper! God hadn't realised his liberator was famous and the accident of meeting and then seeing a picture was marvellous. He read on, delighted at the coincidence. It would be interesting to get in contact so they could talk things over.

God almost spilled his coffee. Below the photograph was a description of his own incident. It was a sensationalist report and the journalist had made no attempt to get to the truth even though survival and renewal were the essence of the story. Nearly four paragraphs? Geezer was described in glowing detail but for some reason the victim barely merited a mention. God reminded himself that inaccuracies were to his advantage and, feeling somewhat pacified, he managed to finish breakfast.

Back in the room, the few remaining chores were easy to organise. The suit was despatched to the laundry, his shoes would need to be polished and the last of the previous day's purchases settled in the wardrobe. He looked around, always more comfortable with order and organisation. There was nothing more to be done.

He took up the briefcase and set off for the bank, thinking how lucky it was to have arranged extra funds even before he had made the critical decision to stay in London.

The weather was good, the forecast remained promising and God decided to brave the trains one more time. Nothing could dent his confidence and in keeping with his mood the tube system suffered no delays. It was only minutes before he found his way to Bond Street station. A short ride on the escalator, a few steps and he was back on the familiar territory of Oxford Street. This time nobody challenged him when he walked into a branch of Waterstones to buy a map.

He sauntered along vaguely noticing the changes since his recent purchase. Ten minutes earlier his passage had been uninterrupted whereas now the pavements were busy and the lights were against him whichever way he turned. It looked as if his luck had run out and doubts crowded in. He had to get the money before the tide turned completely. A decent rainstorm would have cleared the way and provided an excuse to run but he was trapped in the crowd of modern-day hunter gatherers celebrating life with a visit to the shops.

As he approached the bank, he started to anticipate every possibility in case Gabriel had sent someone to intercept him. The Archangel wouldn't come down Himself but it was possible He would have sent Michael, Luke or someone more junior. The building itself was quiet with no sign of unusual activity. Inevitably, there were on-going repairs in the surrounding streets with workmen milling about but God didn't have a choice. He resolved to take the chance. If the labourers had been busy, it would have aroused suspicions but most were standing by as one or two tinkered with the excavations. Nothing at all out of the ordinary.

He walked briskly inside and then had to pause as his eyes adjusted to the gloom. He would need a passport to identify himself and had his documents ready exactly as he had been instructed on the previous day. The teller at the window recognised him and called the manager who ushered God from the queue into a private room.

"Mr Godfrey, we were so worried."

"Has... has something gone wrong?" God asked, his voice wavering with emotion.

"Oh sir, we heard about the terrible accident yesterday. We hope you've made a full recovery."

God was shocked that they should have heard about it. It had been only a small article in one of the morning papers and his name hadn't been mentioned. However, it didn't matter how the news had reached them. The story was now public and he had to move quickly. Every second counted.

"We were going to speak to the police, or at least call the hospital," the manager continued.

The news was getting worse and worse.

"Why would you need to do that?" God asked, clearly he had missed some vital point.

"We saw that you had been taken ill, Mr Godfrey, and we didn't know what to do. We would have kept the money but we weren't sure if you would be..."

God knew it was time to take control. The man was panicking and, today of all days, he didn't have time for anyone else's troubles.

"Thank you for your concern but I'm all right, as you can see. Do you think I could collect the money? I have an appointment to get to." He spoke firmly.

The bank manager pulled himself together. If his customer could be brave, then he should play his part too. It was true that you couldn't believe everything you read in the papers but seeing pictures on television had made the episode seem real. He settled into his seat behind the desk and considered the options. It was obvious that Mr Godfrey was fine. In fact, he looked better than on the previous visit to the bank. That was only yesterday, he was surprised to remember. Then his customer had been drab and old-fashioned whereas now he looked fit and healthy, younger too. Possibly he'd had a haircut? In any case, the manager was pleased to have been able to offer sympathy on behalf of the rest of the staff. The human touch was very important in banking, something everyone should remember.

God coughed gently to encourage the gentleman back on track.

"Mr Godfrey, I'm sorry to inform you that the van has been delayed by heavy traffic and these infernal road improvement schemes. I've checked on its progress and we expect to have your money by two o'clock at the latest."

God took a step backwards as though he had been struck. It was turning into a fiasco but he had to maintain a calm public face. Information like this could mean only one thing. Gabriel was looking for him already.

"Fine, fine," he said in a dull voice. It was as much as he could do to speak at all. "I'll be back this afternoon, if you could have it ready. And thank you for your concern. I'm afraid I was the victim of a prank yesterday. I'm on my way to the hospital to sort out the confusion."

The manager was pleased to have resolved the matter without the anticipated complaint. It probably wouldn't be necessary to check again with head office although someone in his position could never be too careful especially when large sums of cash were involved.

"We close at four today and we'll hold the money until you get in. Or until tomorrow if necessary."

"Thank you," God said and got up to leave. He was surprised when the banker insisted on shaking his hand as if to reassure himself that his client was real and alive. It was definitely a bad sign and God needed to get away. He wasn't sure of his next move but the hospital was the last place he would be going.

CHAPTER TWENTY NINE

GOD WALKED FROM THE BANK INTO UNRELENTING sunshine. It had been naïve to ignore the weather forecast and never again would he make the same mistake. Even an innocent report could be hiding significant information and he reminded himself that the bank manager had said something about seeing the incident on the television news.

Nobody was following as he walked along a narrow side street but it was hours before he could expect the money to arrive. Whatever happened he must avoid drawing attention to himself and it was evident he would have to blend in with the throngs of shoppers.

Without stopping to consider whether these actions were reasonable, God joined the pavement traffic and made his way back to Oxford Street hoping to keep a low profile until it was time to return. It felt awkward to be browsing in a pharmacy and then in a shoe shop. Something bigger was required and Selfridges was an obvious choice, a shop devoted to pleasure where nobody would think of looking for a fugitive.

A clock high above on the façade was signalling the hour as he pushed through the main door into air-conditioning. The entrance led him through a series of boutiques where women of all ages were having their faces decorated by other, equally painted, ladies. The competition of perfumes was difficult to comprehend and he moved on past scarves, handbags and jewellery until he found himself standing at the entrance to the food hall. Still too early to think about lunch.

Selfridges had more than four floors and the merchandise was wondrous, like the street near Primrose Hill only on a galactic scale. It was comforting to know that there were others without shopping bags although it wasn't clear what demons they might be hiding from.

He held his breath as escalators carried him higher in the temple of gratification until he found himself among rows of dainty garments modelled by a succession of naked mannequins. Underclothes, he presumed, although the purpose of the costumes was not clear. Time flew as he examined the problem, scrutinizing fine materials and considering the construction. Each item was intricate and detailed but were they intended to be decorative or functional? Ornamental, he concluded, looking at the patterns.

The few customers were all women although one man affecting boredom waited at the fringes of the display. God knew that he had better do the same. There were many incomprehensible rules in this new society and it would be wise to respect the example, at least until he was a little more sure of what was required.

He took up a position to one side and watched as the youngster stood back, leaning on a railing. After a few minutes a woman moved away from the group gathered around the sales desk and walked towards them. The man clasped the female to his chest before dragging her away by the hand. She looked wistfully back at her friends, waving her brightly coloured shopping bag like a trophy or possibly a good luck charm. God found himself alone and he wasn't sure what to do next. There was no one left to copy and it wasn't clear that he needed one of these young women with or without her charm. He decided to leave before anyone approached.

"Bye-bye," the girls at the till were waving.

To him? He hurried away, relieved at the lucky escape. One moment more and something might have happened. Finding a mate in a shop? He should learn not to be surprised.

There was another hour to wait so he was entitled to eat. In fact, it would be irresponsible not to.

★

Poor Mr Godfrey, she thought, the incident on the television news last night had been awful. If the reports were to be believed, he didn't have family in London. People didn't just disappear and she wondered if he would appreciate a visit while he recuperated. It was no trouble to drop by the hospital. It would take only a few minutes to finish up in Selfridges and she could pop in on her way home. Of course, they had only met briefly and she didn't know him well but that could be a help too. If he gave any sign that her presence were an intrusion, it would be easy enough to leave.

It was a little strange that she had been thinking about him. She looked again at a causally dressed man going through the bras with concentrated attention. Not that there was anything wrong with a man buying underwear, they say most men do. The curious thing was that the shopper bore an uncanny resemblance to Mr Godfrey.

The gentleman had given up his meticulous examination and was leaning against the railing with a man, too young to be married, who was waiting for a girlfriend. The lookalike had been a more active customer and she wondered which of the women in the queue might belong to him. Unlike the teenager, he showed no sign of embarrassment but he was clearly waiting for someone because he kept looking at his watch. Aside from that, he appeared to be enjoying himself.

She paid for her purchases and made her way to the exit. She was looking forward to seeing Mr Godfrey. Hopefully he would remember.

CHAPTER THIRTY

THE BACK STREET GOD HAD CHOSEN WAS ALMOST EMPTY as he walked away from Selfridges. It had been easy to get a snack but he knew there were more troublesome obstacles ahead. In spite of himself he was feeling hopeful. There was something in the air, as if he was not alone, and he set off feeling optimistic.

He took a circuitous route towards the bank looking for the first sign of trouble and taking care whenever he crossed a road. Then he realised that not being alone was a sign that the pursuers were somewhere close. Maybe it wasn't worth trying to get the money at all. The manager would be at lunch or have gone off sick, or another complication would have arisen. And if Gabriel caught up with him? What would happen then? There would be some degree of coercion but surely there would be no violence although such behaviour had become commonplace in modern times. He knew about previous efforts to eliminate wickedness but goodness had always depended on evil as a point of reference and sinful behaviour would be around forever. Like all his schemes, this world was running out of control. Despite the most intricate planning, things went wrong.

It was with a heavy heart that he made his way into the bank for the third and last time. His surprise was obvious as he was again ushered into the private room and presented with his money. No questions were asked although he showed his passport for the sake of formality. The manager was determined to be helpful. He could tell that Mr Godfrey was an important man and he had been kind enough not to complain after all he had been through. Whatever happened, this branch of the banking industry was not going to be criticised for unnecessary red tape and delays.

God walked back into the sunlight carrying the briefcase filled with his life savings, feeling bewildered at the turn of events. Apparently he had side-stepped every problem, almost as though pessimism had come to his aid. However, it was obvious he still needed to be careful. Things seemed to be going well but when he tried to hail a taxi, it failed to stop. The driver looked sharply at him before speeding off although he wasn't aware of any behaviour that flagged him as a potential troublemaker. With no alternative, he took the Tube back to the hotel and his journey was acceptably smooth. He hung tightly on to his case and had the ticket ready when he arrived at Holborn after a minor delay when the train was forced to wait in a tunnel, but it was only for two minutes.

The weather had changed by the time he re-emerged onto the pavement. A light drizzle had cleared the way and the few remaining pedestrians were contented with the return of normal summer. God couldn't help feeling relieved to be back at the hotel. Everything would be all right if he could only manage his expectations.

Alone in his room, he took off his shoes and lay on the bed after what had turned out to be a stressful but productive day. The configurations of an earthly existence were slowly becoming familiar and his thoughts wandered from the airport to the hotel on Portland Place, through illness and uncertainty, until he arrived at the momentous decision to choose an independent life. All events seemed to follow a path that drifted into focus as he progressed through the difficulties and successes of the present day. Starting with breakfast, the delay at the bank, lunchtime and then… he sat up, turning the idea over in his mind. He had passed through a period when the only certainty was rejection. He couldn't help smiling as he uncovered a defined pattern: *the trials of immigration formed a recurring cycle.*

God could see that, like any newcomer, he had brought goals imported from his past and it was these unrealistic expectations that had led to each phase of rejection. The only way for an immigrant to make progress was to choose sensible options. And therein lay the problem. Reasonable behaviour might appear simple but it can be difficult to achieve.

Comparisons between the new life and a glorious past would always end with dissatisfaction, and a *resurrection of old ideals* would always return the immigrant to a *no* phase at the start of another cycle. A thought about the weather might be sufficient, even the hardness of a hotel mattress could be enough to encourage wistfulness for the unrivalled comfort of his old bed back in Heaven.

God realised how lucky he had been. Low expectations had enabled him to get the money from the bank and all the way back to the hotel, but since then something must have happened to move him along the path. The recollection of an incident appeared almost immediately. He had been jostled at the exit from the tube station when he had been a little slow at the ticket barrier. It hadn't struck him as important at the time but he remembered thinking that such rudeness would never have been tolerated in Heaven.

After a series of false turns, the difficulties he faced were finally becoming clear. It was no great leap to appreciate that the suspicious weather and delays at the bank, and even the dark thoughts about compulsion, were simply manifestations of the immigration process and were unlikely to have anything to do with Gabriel. God had to concentrate on getting through the latest round of difficulties so that he was in a phase of *reasonable options* when it was time to make important decisions.

Looking forward, he felt comfortable with his abilities and managed to discount the perils of self-confidence. Crucially, with the discovery of the theory of immigration came a plan for future action. It didn't matter that another *no* phase lurked around the corner, God believed he could handle every detail.

CHAPTER THIRTY ONE

THE SHOWER WAS FUNCTIONAL. THERE WAS DECENT pressure but the water never managed to get much beyond lukewarm. God returned to his tasks. Had the suit been returned from the cleaners? *No.* He tried to telephone the laundry but nobody answered. It was obvious which way things were heading.

He made his way down to the reception desk wearing a mixture of clothes, some wet, some dry, and asked for directions to the restaurant.

"It's closed at the moment," the junior receptionist looked up from her computer screen.

"But I need…" he was going to protest but chose another option. "Can I book a table for dinner?"

"We don't take reservations at this desk. You'll need to do that in the restaurant itself," she managed to answer.

"But you said the restaurant is closed," God could feel his irritation level rising.

"That's correct. I'm afraid you'll have to try later."

"All right," he took the decision to move on. "Can

I get my suit from the cleaners?"

"*No*, sir, I'm sorry. The laundry won't be available until this evening."

God nodded. These requests were not unreasonable and the negative responses could only mean that he was in a phase of rejection.

"What time does it open?" he asked.

"I'm not sure."

God thanked the unsuspecting employee. At least he knew where he stood. To be sure, he tried one more question. It was obvious that in the middle of a *no* phase he would never be able to book the room for an extra night.

The young woman was relieved and delighted to be helpful. *Yes*, of course he could keep the room for another night. For longer if necessary. Would he like to stay until the end of the week?

God needed time to think. A positive response? During rejection? In some way, he must have misunderstood.

The door to his room opened without difficulty but he remained in the corridor pensive yet composed. He replaced the electronic key in his pocket. Actually, the answer was obvious. He had been sure that he wouldn't be able to extend the reservation and it must have been the lack of confidence that had boosted him out of the *no* phase and brought him to a *reasonable option*. It was in line with the pattern, exactly as he had first thought.

He strode into the room feeling smug that the world was at his fingertips. Never again would he have to worry.

"Room service," he said assertively when the operator answered his call.

"I am so sorry, sir, the kitchens are closed for general maintenance."

"Okay. Thank you," God laughed, more out of shame than humour. He had been caught smartly and the latest unhelpful reaction indicated the quickest turn through the cycle yet. With one foolish, overconfident demand he had taken himself directly back to the start of the sequence.

There was no time to lose. The longer he stayed in the negative state, the stronger it would be. He made his way downstairs again. If he were truly correct, the way forward would be to ask the right questions, to ask for things no-one in their right mind could deny. It might be humiliating but this was a state of emergency and there was nothing else that he could do.

It was raining outside, clear to anyone who cared to look.

"Is it raining?" he inquired tentatively.

"Yes," the doorman wasn't sure what to make of the question. "It undoubtedly is."

God opened his umbrella and prepared to set off along the pavement. So far so good, he thought. The Tube station was close, only fifty yards away.

"Can you direct me to the Underground?" he asked, in no doubt about the answer.

"Certainly," the confused young man answered, pointing the way along the street. "In this direction. Two minutes, sir, it's very close."

God wondered whether the answer counted. At least the adolescent fellow was being helpful. He made his way along the pavement trying to think of questions that might help but it didn't take long to have second thoughts. Just because somebody says yes...

"Can I buy a magazine?" he asked a Big Issue salesman sheltering in a doorway. The man was in his mid-thirties, unshaven, with a dog.

"Yes, of course," came the answer, but he wasn't so sure when God proffered a £50 note. "*No* mate, *no*. I've got no change."

"Oh, you can keep the change if you'll say yes,"

God assured him.

"Yes, yes, yes. And thanks," the vendor couldn't help thinking about the strange people you met on the streets. In London and everywhere else.

God's programme should have been going well but he felt silly standing in the downpour with a wet magazine. If the cycle was as powerful as he imagined, a silly tactic wasn't going to help. He chose the *reasonable option*, turned on his heel and walked back to the hotel.

It must have worked because things were different once he made his way through the entrance. The doorman smiled and the receptionist greeted him.

"Hello, sir. I've located your clothes and the restaurant is back on line. Shall I book a table for 8.30?"

Not wishing to upset the balance God agreed with every suggestion and returned to the room with his suit. It was pressed and clean, in perfect order. He was pleased but was careful to moderate the appreciation. Whatever happened he didn't want to lose newly reclaimed *reason* too quickly.

CHAPTER THIRTY TWO

It was God's first free day since the big decision and with no particular duties to fulfil it was inevitable that he should consider his position and devote time to planning for the future. There had been mishaps along the way but he had made progress and most of the complications appeared to be under control. He spoke English, was educated, intelligent and well-informed, and he even had a passport stamped with indefinite leave to remain. Looking at the situation with a rational eye, it was clear that there was nothing specific to complain about. On the other hand, there was nothing to be gained by pretending he fitted in. The feeling of disquiet hovered tenuously. Nobody could be tired of London – that wouldn't be reasonable – but he realised he was experiencing the lack of reassurance that comes from being established and among familiar things. He took care when thinking about Heaven and avoided anything that could be construed as reminiscence.

The time had come to begin a new life, and yet

there was nothing to take his mind off the awful emptiness that stretched ahead. He couldn't help himself. He might have been unhappy in Heaven, frustrated even, but he had never had to contend with troubles like this. The trappings of existence had been stripped away and he was faced with the raw prospect of his own future. Progress ground to a halt.

What is worth doing? he asked himself. It was the most fundamental of questions but the more he concentrated, the more slippery the answers became, drifting through his fingers and evading every grasp. Leaving the abstract behind, God found a seat at a pavement café and ordered coffee. Practical choices must lead the way forward.

Education was an obvious path for any newcomer and sitting before the computer screen in the local public library, he considered an application for university. He imagined sending a form with no school record, no exam results and even fewer referees. It was a proposal destined for failure and if he had learnt nothing else it was that wishful thinking was guaranteed to be unproductive. In any case, living with teenagers would present challenges God couldn't imagine being pleasant. Heaven had never defined an age but mid-life seemed most appropriate for someone in his position, and experience must count for something even in this relentless world.

More basic was the problem of money. Unless he found a job, he would run out of funds and the choices would be stark. Go back to Heaven with his tail between his legs or... or what? The prospects of homelessness and beggary weren't worth contemplating. His clothes were still damp and he had only been in the rain for five minutes.

What would he do if he were destitute? Perhaps this was the way to approach the problem. What if he had no money and nowhere to stay? Try as he might, it was impossible to pretend to be desperate. He would have to move forward from where he was, not from some hypothetical point. There would always be people worse off than himself.

God approached the problem with characteristic determination. He found a piece of paper and a pencil and made a list of practicalities to keep his mind on track. At the top of the page was finding employment. Second would have to be accommodation. He could stay in a hotel for the time being but eventually he would have to find somewhere permanent. Terraced houses materialised in his thoughts, leading inevitably to Regent's Park and the people he had met when he had first arrived. His *lady friend* as the gatekeeper had called her – but it was wrong to describe her in such terms, and she wouldn't be interested in an immigrant with no prospects. She had been happy last time they had met, with her job, her son and that confusing business of a partner. He still had the card with her number in his wallet but it would have to go. An unreachable ideal would send him back to rejection and the temptation would be too great.

Who else did he know? The girl, his favourite receptionist at the first hotel, and Confucius who could be relied on for advice even if it was usually difficult to understand. It was obvious that this too was a blind alley. His oldest friend had made a fresh start and would be impossible to find; there could be thousands of motorcycle couriers in London. Which meant that for the moment he was entirely on his own. Stifling regret as much he could manage, he dropped the taxi driver's card in a bin, and set off to begin his search.

After a long day, God headed back to the hotel to use the telephone before low spirits could take hold. The search for a job had begun in a mood of reasonable optimism but finding someone who would take him seriously was proving difficult.

In the quiet of his bedroom, he looked once more through the newspapers. There were many positions advertised, and each one required references or evidence of skills and qualifications. He wasn't expecting to be a doctor but law should have been an easy choice. Cosmology was a possibility but if he couldn't get an interview, how could he show that he had something useful to contribute?

There was no way of getting the required experience and it was becoming obvious that ambition was damaging his chances. The next day, when he started again, he would look lower down on the earnings register.

Altogether, it had been a busy day and he was relieved to still have a place to stay. He examined himself in the mirror, wondering if he should dress for dinner and whether the uniform of modern clothing could have anything to do with the way he felt. The salesman might have dressed him in the latest fashions but inside he was different. In any case, the process of immigration was a cycle which meant success would come eventually. He put aside plans for the restaurant and tried room service. To his relief, he found that it was working.

"*No*, sir, I'm sorry. *No* eggs and bacon at this hour," a young man answered the phone. The electronic sound of a video game could be heard in the background. "Can I help you with anything else?"

Would these trials never cease? God took time to think, a strategy was needed to get himself through this tricky patch.

"All right," he kicked off his shoes and climbed onto the bed. "Tell me what is available." He hadn't even asked a question which meant he stood a decent chance of making progress.

"Don't you have a menu, sir?"

It was a trick. If he said *yes*, the boy at the end of the line would ask him what he wanted again, and they would be back to square one.

"*No*," God said and waited calmly for the response.

"We can arrange anything you want, sir, anything at all."

"But you said I can't have breakfast," he answered smartly.

"It's tea time and most people…"

"Forgive me, young man, but I am not 'most people'," God caught himself in mid-sentence. There was no reason to get into an argument. "What kind of sandwiches do you have?"

"Cheese, tomato, ham…"

"That will be fine. I'll have a cheese, tomato and ham sandwich. And a pot of tea."

"What kind of bread would you like?" the youth was asking.

"Please choose for me. Anything will be fine," God countered, smiling to himself.

The young man admitted defeat and repeated the order with grudging respect, even offering extra salad and fries.

It was done. The disagreement had been unnecessary and he should have remembered that the employee may have been struggling with his own cycle of rejection. The trouble was that he was tired and this wasn't the time for sympathy.

While he was waiting, God sat down in front of the television to get an update on the news. He was particularly keen to see how his own story was evolving. There was a longish report on the local channel. Geezer was still not commenting but there was a video taken by a passing tourist, on a mobile phone apparently, showing an elderly man having his chest pummelled in the street. From nowhere, a crowd had gathered to greet the arrival of the ambulance with a cheer. No wonder the bank manager had been concerned. To God, sitting comfortably in the hotel room, none of it looked real.

The main news began, not a single item to do with London, and he daydreamed while images of war and disaster beamed into the room from around the globe. The stories were depressingly familiar but the pictures of trauma were getting increasingly graphic. Someone needed to help the world back towards respectability.

The thought was sobering. Was that what he wanted, to be back in Heaven, tinkering with the system? Not really, he concluded. He missed the company but that was all. For many years Gabriel and his team had been searching for a solution to the problem of pain and suffering but there wasn't anything to be done. Not from Heaven anyway, and there was even less chance of making progress down on Earth. It was arrogance to think one could make a difference.

Supper arrived and he signed the chit, wondering whether to give a tip. It wasn't the same person delivering the food but he couldn't help feeling guilty about the telephone argument. After a brief tussle with his conscience, he settled down in front of the TV with the tray on his lap and was in time to catch the end of a police interview. A picture appeared onscreen followed by a telephone number – the only discussion he needed to see and it was gone.

He did his best to remain calm, reminding himself that it was going to be tricky navigating without ideals and easy to be thrown off course. There would be news on other channels and he needed to learn to control his temper. Too many years of too many people singing his praises, he thought, and clearly he had become dependent. This world was very different. His expectations might be for adoration but nobody was interested anymore.

The picture was back on the screen. An angelic-looking official, plainly Michael in disguise, was asking for information concerning the whereabouts of Mr. Godwin Godfrey, who had been resuscitated on the roadside in Marylebone and had then disappeared from hospital. They were showing the dramatic scenes as Geezer in his dirty working clothes leaned over the elderly figure performing artificial respiration while others looked on. The taste of onions returned and God pushed away the plate of food. Once again, there was the photograph.

"If anyone has information on the whereabouts…"

The picture was hardly a good likeness. He didn't feel old but presumably they thought differently about him in Heaven. Michael wasn't much good as a policeman either.

The report didn't mention the bank but they must know by now. The manager would have called their hotline. It was with relief that he realised the corollary of all the publicity – if they were still looking, then they didn't yet know where he was. Confucius and a visit to the old hotel were completely out of the question.

He took up his sandwich again and was lost in thought as he flicked through the range of channels, bypassing adult entertainment and moving on to holiday programmes. Far enough from his own experiences to give him peace and send him quickly off to sleep.

A NEW BEGINNING

CHAPTER THIRTY THREE

A YEAR HAD PASSED AND GOD WAS AT EASE AS HE prepared breakfast with the Today programme whispering in his ear for company.

The political haranguing was of little interest but it was better than the bleating of the television or the lonely silence that were the only alternatives. He remembered his early experiences with radio fondly and it gave him pleasure to think of Broadcasting House not far down the road.

It had been a testing period but he had come to an accommodation with the world. Barring a few flashes of anger and the inevitable consequences, he had settled into a long *reasonable options* phase. He had learned not to worry and to be less concerned with the dignity of his position. His first job had been in a sandwich shop in a side street off New Fetter Lane.

After a few months behind the counter, he'd had a stroke of luck. A chance conversation while he was mixing mayonnaise had taken an unexpected turn and his knowledge of world events had landed him a job as a researcher in a press agency. The position was nothing grand but he looked forward to each day, mostly to seeing the enthusiasm with which the youngsters in the office approached every new disaster. He had too much experience to get involved but he loved to watch them work, tension running high as if the world was going to end. It would have been a pity to muddy the waters with cynicism, so he didn't. In fact, he seldom said a word unless there was ancient or classical history to be clarified. Mostly he enjoyed the atmosphere and kept his head down.

The last big *no* phase had taken it out of him. He didn't want to go through that again so he stuck to his job and tinkered with his flat. With his capital and his earnings, which improved marginally from time to time, he managed reasonably well. He had come to know Regent's Park, and Primrose Hill was now as familiar as a friend. He seldom strayed off his patch.

A few months back, his comrade from the hotel, the motorcycle courier, had given a curious interview on television. He had formed a successful partnership with the eastern potentate who had been at Heathrow on the day of God's arrival; the stock market was soaring and in due course a book would be published with a description of their investment strategy. God could already imagine what it would be – a short self-help volume with valuable but incomprehensible advice. Nobody but the authors would be able to translate the principles into a winning programme but it would probably sell well enough. God wondered if these things were part of a plan for re-settlement and whether Confucius had to go through the cycle each time he took on a new persona. Probably not, since adjusting to immigration is a question of expectations and that couldn't have anything to do with the particular body you occupy at one time.

God had thought about rebirth and reincarnation, wondering whether being younger would have conferred any advantage. The strange thing was that he felt more youthful as time passed. He had left his responsibilities behind in Heaven, and it showed.

Thought for the Day arrived, a spot that served only as a timekeeper. He was still brushing his teeth which meant he was behind in his routine. Not that it was essential but he liked to arrive at the office with the other workers even if his expertise wasn't usually required so early in the morning. Still, one never knew. Jerusalem may be rediscovered in Kent or some galleon unearthed in the Costa Smeralda. It was an enticing prospect and an excuse to go away before the school holidays started.

He caught himself daydreaming and looked at the time. The newsreader was done with the headlines and he wasn't nearly ready. Not that clothes were a problem. He had settled into a style that was probably old-fashioned but the important thing was that he was able to relax. A suit, dark shoes, everything was off-the-peg regulation stuff. Nowadays, he didn't have to please anyone but himself.

After a brief look around, he took up his briefcase and set off on foot. For months he had been following the same route through Fitzrovia and Bloomsbury then down Chancery Lane to work. The last time he had needed a car was after the Christmas party when he had twisted an ankle trying to do some or other dance intended for people younger than himself. He hadn't been very good but his colleagues had been noticeably pleased. For them it was light-hearted and fun but he knew he had to be careful with the ups and downs of the immigration cycle and was wary about what he hoped for. The few drinks had been a risk, even so it had turned out all right. He had probably watched too many television movies over the holidays but at least he had been able to put his feet up and the leg had healed quickly.

The day felt a little strange as he walked along. He hadn't had a reflective mood like this in ages. Something to do with the anniversary, no doubt. He felt a drop on his shoulder. It had started to rain and he had forgotten to bring an umbrella.

A taxi was an obvious solution but he already knew how things would work. Any available cab driver would pass by and choose the girls who were using the usual tricks to jump the queue. The blonde hair, God reflected, works every time. He was dowdy by comparison and wouldn't complain. The drivers deserved any excitement they could get and good luck to them if a passenger livened up their day.

He didn't bother to raise a hand to the next cab, admitting defeat as three young women danced around to attract attention. He made no move even when the taxi pulled up nearby causing the girls to run in a welter of flying skirts and scarves, heels tapping along the pavement. He knew that he would be in danger if he tried too hard or hoped for even this one small thing. He might be an established immigrant but the *no* phase could take him yet.

The driver seemed to be beckoning.

"You wanted a taxi, didn't you?"

God looked up. The voice was so familiar.

"Come on, jump in. I can't keep the baying hounds away forever."

The shrieking group was almost upon them. God opened the door.

"You look different," he said.

"I wondered if you would remember me," she caught his eye in the rear view mirror.

He blushed. "I didn't know…"

"Did you want to go somewhere or were you simply loitering?"

"I'm on my way to work but you know what it's like when it starts raining. The young girls always get picked up first."

"Leaving the mature gentlemen behind for us ladies," she looked amused.

He said nothing, lost in thought. His reserve was in danger of being shattered. He had never allowed himself to hope that they would meet again.

"… Well?"

"I'm sorry?"

"Do you want me to drive around aimlessly or can I take you where you're going?"

"I… ah… my office is on Fleet Street," he said.

The silence was companionable rather than

awkward and it was some while before God spoke.

"I've thought about you often." The simple statement of a true fact couldn't threaten his status.

"And I you," she smiled.

They were on Kingsway nearing the courts before either said another word and then they both started together.

"Me first," God said, "before my courage fails."

She nodded. They could drive up and down the road until he was ready.

"Can I see you again? Forgive me, I mean more than once every year." It was a giant leap and he hoped she wouldn't be offended.

"I'd like that." She waited to see if there was anything more.

"This is where I work. Time does fly."

She pulled up near the Goldman building and God hesitated before climbing out. He reached for his money.

"Don't be silly," she laughed.

He didn't know what to say next.

"Where?" she was asking.

He looked blank.

"Where do you want to meet?" she said again.

"Oh, I see." He thought for a moment. "I don't

know my way around very well. What about… could we go to Primrose Hill?"

It was done. He had asked and she had agreed to his suggestion for the weekend. God wasn't sure what would happen next. It could be that he had chosen a *reasonable option*, or that she was *ideal*. Anything too ambitious could lead back to the *no* phase but it didn't matter. He knew it was worth the risk. If he hadn't been impetuous and thrown away her card, he could easily have called before.

The world felt very different after the short taxi journey. Godfrey arrived at the agency a touch early but positively skipping up the steps and into the glass atrium. Not one of his co-workers could believe this was the same man whose devotion to the ancient world had previously overridden all traces of enthusiasm for the pleasures of modern life. It caused a few comments – nothing racy, but everyone was pleased to see a colleague looking happy.

He didn't mind what they said. They would settle down once they started working and he would be left to thoughts that for the first time in a year were hopeful and enthusiastic.

Unfortunately, the day was turning out to be quiet.

There were a few minor food disasters and the usual complaints about the health service but there was nothing substantial to provide distraction. The open-plan office, filled with journalists, was buzzing with anticipation at the prospect of an in-house story. It was obvious that something had happened. Old Godfrey was much more animated than usual. He had been caught in the rain like everyone else but this was more than a simple soaking. He was at his desk chuckling as he looked through the internal emails, and the jokes doing the circuit were never that funny.

Idle hands and the absence of tension in the world were leading to a dangerous level of chatter. By the time Godfrey took his first break of the morning and strolled down the aisle to stretch his legs, speculation was running rife. No-one had yet been brave enough to broach the subject. It would have to be one of his small circle of intimates, one of those who had confessed to him over the past few months.

It had turned out to be useful having someone older on the team. People could let off steam knowing their senior colleague wasn't participating in the incestuous fraternisation that beset any organisation filled with bright-young-things. Men and women had spoken to Godfrey from time to time about their little difficulties, knowing he would treat their confidences with the discretion they deserved. Sometimes they deserved more, sometimes less, and he always tried to do his best for his young friends even if it required a hint to one or other party that interest had been expressed or that willingness would be reciprocated. No one had ever imagined that, one day, he would be in need of a similar service.

God couldn't concentrate so it was lucky most of his work could be done without serious thought. Messages found their way, unbidden, to his computer. There was seldom anything relevant but he read every note before filing or deleting each in turn. The new day was the same; sunshine in Newfoundland, jewels in Petra, expanding ice sheets in Antarctica. Then lost property and the usual selection of humour. He clicked on the junk folder and the last was gone, leaving a neat and tidy inbox.

CHAPTER THIRTY FOUR

GOD LOOKED AROUND THE OFFICE. A SURGE OF INTEREST was sweeping through the big room, leaping from desk to desk like a salmon. As an outsider, he often had difficulty anticipating which minor story was going to inflate. For something like that the agency relied on the stable of young newshounds; with their noses to the ground they could sniff a scandal at any distance. It was probably something to do with one of the dispatches he had already consigned to the dustbin.

The computer pinged. Messages were arriving in his inbox. He could never understand why people sent emails when they could speak across the desk. He looked up and waved to the sender of the latest missive.

"I'm fine, thanks, Rebecca," he said. "And how are you?"

"All good, so far. Not much to keep us busy," Rebecca smiled. If Godfrey wanted to say something that would be fine but people were entitled to their private happiness. He had never burdened them with problems and he must have had his share. The press agency suited him but for a wise old gentleman to have been selling sandwiches... well, he must have had bad luck along the way.

"Same for me." He would have liked to chat, there was a lot to think about before the weekend and it would be nice to talk things over. Still, he wasn't sure whether to say anything. At his time of life people would expect him to be in control and he didn't want to cause problems. "Nothing unusual."

Rebecca turned back to her work but she kept up with the wave of gossip that was gathering momentum. The consensus of opinion was that Godfrey's new-found happiness could only be explained by a relationship. Nobody knew who it could be but it didn't really matter. Somebody had caught his eye and good luck to him.

"Hmm," he said, yawning and humming as he read stories from around the world, speculating about where the next big thing was coming from.

"Is everything all right? You're distracted today," she said.

"Am I? Oh dear." He clicked on a link and sharpened a pencil while the page opened.

She waited for him to continue but he was back in

his thoughts wondering about the state of his clothes and whether he should wear something different on the weekend.

"I missed what you said."

"Oh." Godfrey looked up, his colleague was waiting for him to speak. He must have been thinking aloud. "Sorry, I was daydreaming."

There was nothing more she could do. If he'd give no clues, she'd best mind her own business and concentrate on work.

"Um, Rebecca, could I ask you something?" Godfrey said in a low voice leaning towards her across the desk.

Rebecca could feel the hush, the entire office appeared to be listening in.

She knew where loyalty lay and her profession was instantly sacrificed in the name of friendship. She reached for the keyboard and tapped out a message that appeared instantly in Godfrey's inbox.

`Let's have a coffee. ;-)`

Why couldn't she say this out loud? But God didn't want to appear old-fashioned and he replied in kind, slowly spelling out his note.

Re:
Message from Godfrey.
Thank you, that would be nice.
Sincerely. Godfrey

Send.

Already, there was another message in the inbox.

Open.
Re: Re:
C U *bucks in 10

Reply to Sender.
Re: Re: Re:
Message from Godfrey.
Do you mean the usual Starbucks
on Fleet Street?

Send.

She must be in the middle of something. He
shouldn't have disturbed her but there was no time to
ask because she had already left the office with only
the briefest of smiles in his direction. Which of the

circulating stories was she working on? He patted his pockets to make sure he had everything and set off to meet her across the road.

The cafe was empty after the morning rush and it was hours to go before lunch.

"Hiya," she said, as he stepped inside.

"Hello, Rebecca, what can I get for you?" It had become a habit for him to buy the drinks.

"My turn today," she announced and jumped up to the counter before he had a chance to protest.

"Cup of tea for me," he called after her. Hopefully he hadn't taken her away from anything important. They could have talked in the office easily enough.

He settled back to wait wondering how his little question had developed into a clandestine meeting. Oh well, he thought, it was a special day. His routine was out the window but this was definitely preferable, frightening and hopeful in equal measure.

"Thanks," he said when she returned with two steaming mugs. After the morning's storm, it was exactly what he needed.

She settled next to him so that they could watch the passers-by on the pavement and talk without the pressure of enforced eye contact. As usual, Godfrey was reluctant to get started. He didn't have much to say about himself as a rule. They had always talked about her when they slipped out of the office for a quick coffee. Maybe, she thought, he needed a bit of help to get going.

"Why are you called Godfrey?" she asked.

"Oh, I suppose because it's my name," he said with a twinkle in his eye.

"I know that but nobody uses surnames these days."

"That's true," he laughed, so much more cheerful than usual. "I could call you Standfast if you like."

"Oh please, it sounds ridiculous."

"Good, I like the name Rebecca."

"Thanks, but I was thinking you must have a Christian name."

"Godwin, I suppose."

"Godwin Godfrey?" This wasn't turning out as she had expected but at least he was chatting.

"Sounds strange, doesn't it? At one time I thought I would be 'Jeremy' but that didn't last very long," he sipped his tea pensively.

"Oh, I see, a nickname from when you were younger," she fished a bar of chocolate from her handbag and offered him a piece.

"What do you mean?"

"Is that what they called you at work? Before you came to us?"

"Not really. I used to be called 'God'," he said before he could stop himself. And couldn't help blushing at the thought.

"Oh, that's great! It really suits you. I must tell them back at the office," she put an excited hand on his arm but stopped when she saw his face. "Don't worry, I'll keep it confidential. You would have said something before if you had wanted us to know."

She was right. He had never told anybody about himself and how could you be friendly without offering such basic information?

Rebecca waited anxiously until he looked up. She was supposed to be helping.

"It's not a secret. Nobody's ever asked me, that's all," he held the cup tightly to steady his hand.

"Anyway, you couldn't introduce yourself with a title like that," she chuckled. "People would have unrealistic expectations. Good Heavens... ha ha... look at the time, I'm going to be late for morning briefing. See you back at the office."

God watched her hurrying along the pavement. So much for the question, he thought, but he had enjoyed his tea and the chat. There was no hurry, he could always get advice later on.

Everything had changed by the time he made it back to the office. God sorted through his desktop to see if there was anything for him to work on. The Balkan flare-up looked dangerous and Africa was a powder keg as usual. Nothing particularly new but the modern media brought the stories home and made every threat tangible. Minutes before, he had felt so happy but the problems came flooding back as he sat looking at the computer. The only comfort was that people were doing well aside from headline events, and were mostly happier and living longer. It was clear that Gabriel was managing.

Back in the world of work, the historical connections between the warring factions in the Middle East occupied his attention for the next few hours. He was determined to keep moralising and conjecture from his professional life but it was a subject close to his heart. Without breaking confidences, he tried to set the story on an accurate historical footing, leaving it to the leader writers to propose ethical judgements or to make a persuasive case.

He surfaced from the mayhem wondering how a conflict that had spanned thousands of years could generate deadlines in terms of hours. It was a story that would go on forever but artificial time pressures cranked up the tension and got the team working efficiently. All of a sudden he noticed that messages were reaching him at a new email address. god1world@gmail.com had seemed so natural that he hadn't broken step.

He looked over at Rebecca who was still buried in her work. Her version of discretion was to tell everyone, not only their co-workers in the office but also the rest of the modern world. In a way he was pleased the secret was finally out in the open.

```
Message from God to Standfast.
All of a sudden the world knows
about me. I wonder how it
happened?
G
```

He clicked and the message was on its way. It wasn't his first foray into the world of electronic communications but it was the first from the new address. She must have arranged it through one of her friends in the IT department.

CHAPTER THIRTY FIVE

"MICHAEL," GABRIEL SAID. "COME IN WHEN YOU'RE READY."

"Good morning. Not much to report," the interim-archangel opened the door and took his usual seat. It was true barring his one big case. After the chaos of the early months, Heaven had settled down. Gabriel had grown into His role with great authority and now no-one had a surer touch. That brought Michael back to his only preoccupation – it was exactly one year and he still hadn't been able to find God. Strangely, Gabriel had never given any sign of being worried.

"No, Mike, I'm not upset and not surprised either. Before he left he gave strict instructions about not making contact and it's Our duty to obey orders. He'll reveal himself when he wants to come home."

"Of course, You're right. I didn't intend to question Your judgement."

"Let's get on with the job. What do you want to tell Me? Any new leads?"

"Only one… actually, there are two. I'm not sure,"

Michael said carefully. There was no chance of hiding anything from Gabriel.

"All right, carry on."

"I found a new address, email, that he might be using. Godonearth or something like that. Might be of interest."

"And the other?"

"The woman who came looking for him at the hospital. I'm sure you remember the taxi driver? The one who was so concerned," Michael couldn't conceal his fervour.

"I thought you had seen her and found that she had no connection," Gabriel yawned.

"I did and she didn't, not really anyway. She drove him to that hotel, the first one, and then denied all knowledge of his whereabouts."

"So?" the atmosphere darkened, Gabriel could feel Himself getting impatient.

"So I kept an eye on her," nothing would stop Michael and he continued with unrelenting zeal. "She's booked herself into a hairdresser."

"Oh come on. There's nothing suspicious in that. Lots of women have their hair cut." Gabriel forced Himself to relax. As usual, His deputy was overdoing it, burning conspiracies behind every bush.

THE UNIVERSAL THEORY OF IMMIGRATION

"Aha, this is different. She usually goes on the weekend and now she's made an appointment in the middle of the week," Michael had his moment of triumph. "It's a change of pattern. Could be significant."

"Who else are you checking on? I can't believe you haven't got better things to do," Gabriel was wondering how long this would continue. "I keep telling you, he'll call when he wants Us."

"You also told me I could try to find him, so that's what I'm doing. Surely You don't want me to stop looking?"

What could Gabriel say? He should have kept His mouth shut in the first place. Not that God's absence had made any particular difference. The angels were content, days were much like one another and nobody worried any more that their old leader was out of sight. Only the long-haired Geldof had been a troublemaker and Michael had dealt with him months ago. Peter hadn't been pleased but the fuss was settling down. As for the rest, the world took care of itself. If there were no new miracles, people concentrated on natural wonders or talked of a golden age that had passed. It didn't matter who sat behind the desk in Central Office. Heaven was simply an ideal.

A NEW BEGINNING

God had told Gabriel not to interfere which meant He would have to go on hoping that Michael had no success. So far it had worked but Gabriel couldn't help wishing the ordeal would be over soon.

And as He thought…

CHAPTER THIRTY SIX

GOD HAD NO TIME FOR THE TRAFFIC AND CONFUSION as he set off on foot along Fleet Street in pouring rain. Never mind what clothes he should wear on the weekend, there were more important issues to deal with. The strategy of avoidance had been a failure, he had to pursue *ideals* and give them their head otherwise his time would be completely wasted. It was obvious now but it had taken a year to realise that he had to face his problems head on even if it meant dealing with one more *no* phase. To break the cycle he would have to stop being an immigrant and commit to a single future instead of hoarding options like a refugee.

What should he do? The last time he had been confronted with the question he had resorted to practicalities leaving philosophy aside in an attempt to get on. The immigration cycle had been slowed but it wasn't beaten, as if the iron grip had a velvet glove. There would be no hiding this time. He would deal with whatever obstacles were thrown in his path. Either that or he would fail. It would be better than being in limbo.

He was soaked by the time he passed Fitzroy Square. The gloom was unrelenting but determination drove him onwards. His strategy was to hide no longer and he carried on walking. If it rained, it rained.

The downpour had eased by the time he reached Marylebone, and Regent's Park was clean and clear. At any other time this would have been a sign, a portent, even a good omen, but God no longer had time for such notions. He strode purposefully up the avenue of the formal gardens and was pleased to have reached this point at last. He felt ready to meet his former colleagues, something he hadn't contemplated seriously since the day of the resuscitation near Portland Place.

On he marched, over the pedestrian crossing at the Inner Circle and then up the gentle rise towards the zoo. Before long he was heading downhill towards Prince Albert Road. The thrill of anticipation was inescapable as Primrose Hill came into view.

The drizzle receded but there were few others about. God recognised the hardy souls in their baggy trousers and Birkenstocks as fellow pilgrims, though surely none could have a mission like his. Green fields opened up ahead and his resolve strengthened as the clouds broke, late afternoon light bathing the summit in golden sunshine. He was fitter than when he had first arrived and barely noticed the gradient as he pushed upwards towards the peak.

Ignoring the rain-soaked ground, he chose a seat on the benches near the place where he had slept so long ago. He sat down and surveyed the dominions watched over by Primrose Hill.

"Gabriel," God said.

"Here, Sir," came the immediate reply.

"It's been a while, hasn't it? A little longer than We thought." Not that He had been harbouring doubts but He was pleased to find His assistant as attentive as always. He hadn't particularly wanted to make the journey to Heaven but Gabriel needed to talk face-to-face. He looked around. The office was unchanged, as though no-one had used it the whole year.

"Thank You, Sir. It's truly wonderful to see You again. You said not to interfere so I've been keeping a low profile. Michael has been quite a nightmare," Gabriel hoped God hadn't caught cold sitting on the wet bench on Primrose Hill.

"Don't worry about Me, I'm fine," God laughed.

272

"We have a lot to talk about. I've made a few decisions."

Oh dear, Gabriel was thinking, *I hope He isn't going to be angry*. Too late, he remembered it was the *status quo ante* and his opinions would be on display.

"Never mind," God spoke thoughtfully. The angel's relief was indisputable and God realised He had neglected to consider the effects of His journey on the host of Heaven. Gabriel had obviously been suffering from the awkward position in which he had been left, ostensibly in charge but tied to the oscillations of emotions raging down below on Earth. "Things will get back to normal shortly. At the very least, We'll decide what normal should be and then We can get on with it. After the time you've had, I'm sure you need to let off steam."

Gabriel wondered what was in store.

"It's clear We can't carry on like this," God pressed ahead. "Let's deal with the consequences of these alterations. Tell Me exactly what you think and don't worry about formalities."

The Old Leader was back in charge. Gabriel could only sit and gape as God sketched His new vision which would be all that was the case.

"What do you think?" He asked.

"I'm not sure I understand," Gabriel said, but

thoughts betrayed him. He could see plainly enough that God was no longer in the picture. The *theory of immigration* was all very well for explaining a newcomer's experiences but where did it leave the angels, Gabriel wondered. What about Michael and the rest of them?

"That's up to you," God cut in. "I'm not going to make decisions any more. We are all going to grow up and take responsibility."

"But what's going to happen to Heaven? Are we shutting down?" Gabriel couldn't see a future for himself at all.

"I know it's hard," God said more gently. "It will take some adjustment but you need to get used to change. I've been through all these things Myself over the past year."

"Please, don't do it." Gabriel was close to tears.

"In the end, everyone will be happy. It was the same for Me."

"No, it's not. It's completely different!" Gabriel's voice rose in desperation.

"How so?" God asked patiently. This was a new Him and He knew it was important to bring His underlings along instead of dispensing fiats and expecting them to obey. Gabriel was incoherent but he would come round with a little persuasion. They had all the time in the world.

"You *chose* to go," Gabriel said, collecting himself as best he could. "It was easy for you because You had an objective in mind."

"I didn't know what it was when I first set off. I went on your advice," God reminded him. "But if things work out, when all this is done, at least I'll know where to look."

"Exactly," Gabriel said.

"I'm not following. Come on, old friend, explain to Me what's going on."

"We're happy up here. This is our home so it would be our ideal to come back, only Heaven wouldn't exist any more," Gabriel struggled with his words. "You can go through Your immigration cycle and find Your way but there will be no hope for us. We'll be stuck with rejection and disappointment forever."

God had to admit it was true. Life on Earth didn't suit everyone. There were so many who'd been miserable.

"I see what you mean," He said. "Any ideas about what We should do?"

He knew what the angel was thinking.

"You should come home," Gabriel insisted, although he could already see it was hopeless.

"You know that's not going to happen. Everything has changed, Gabriel. There's no going back."

"But why? Why do You have to force us to come with You?"

Good point. God thought about the alternatives.

"Okay, how about this? We'll straighten things out so that you and Michael have no misunderstandings, then you can go back to whatever you've been doing for the past year while I get on with My new life. Everything will be the same except Michael won't be chasing Me."

"We could do that if You want." Gabriel wasn't going to say anything more. God might be the One making decisions at this particular time, but once He had gone the angels would be in charge. They could easily call God back if they wanted to.

"You've got the wrong idea. We have to agree before I go. You can have anything you want," God offered an olive branch.

"Except the one thing I need," Gabriel retorted.

"There's no need to sulk. Do you remember what you told me before I left? – *Miracles aren't necessary anymore, people are getting on fine without assistance* – I didn't understand at the time, but you were right."

He waited for Gabriel but no sign was forthcoming.

"I suppose there will still be people who need

something to aim for and Heaven will be waiting. It's just that it will be you in charge instead of Me," God said eventually. "Over the past year, while you were directing proceedings, would I have done anything differently?"

"I don't know. Probably not," Gabriel spoke mournfully. It was the end of an era. Nothing would change on Earth but Heaven would feel different. "I have to be able to ask for advice."

"Whenever you think it's necessary," the relieved Deity couldn't help smiling. "All right then, I suppose We'd better speak to Michael together."

The angel Michael arrived, shaken to find himself in the central office when he thought the hunt was winding down.

"I'm leaving for good, Michael," God announced.

"What are You saying?"

"Gabriel can fill you in on the details. I'm sorry you were dragged into this but I needed some time to Myself," He said and sat back waiting for the inevitable response.

"Gabriel knew?" Michael was incandescent. Thunderbolts were flying and, down below, on Primrose Hill, even the most determined dog walkers were leaving in search of shelter.

"Calm down, it would be better to…"

It didn't matter what anybody said, Michael needed time to work through a mountain of frustration. What irked him most was the mirth as Gabriel and God recalled his performance as a nurse and then as a policeman. *He had always liked dressing up.* Very funny. At least he had made the effort.

"Mike, come on. You have to admit your hospital performance was special. I wasn't much better with My hiking boots and that backpack," God knew it was time to move forward. "I admit I had no clue what I was doing either."

"And when You went into the church and demanded attention. What did You say?… Oh yes. 'Don't You know who I am?'," Michael laughed but the others didn't follow. "That was pretty funny too. I suppose You enjoyed being kissed by that Geezer?"

It was God's turn to be upset. He didn't want every paranoid step pored over. He knew He had been stupid but these weren't hanging offences. He deserved a fresh start and He didn't want them looking into His private life too closely, now or in the future.

Gabriel played the peacemaker and gradually the storm cleared. What would happen if things didn't work out, Michael wanted to know? If the world needed a fully functioning team in Heaven after all?

"I don't think that's going to happen," God said. "When you look back over thousands of years, We haven't done very much. Things have been done in Our name, good and bad, but when have We actually made a difference?"

"Not since the Beginning," Gabriel said reflectively. He was thinking about something God had said earlier. Unwittingly, they were stumbling towards something new – a fundamental force that would rival gravity, capitalism and numbers in power.

Perhaps, Gabriel thought, it was something he could work on when God was gone. *Introduction of the New* had always created tension, be it in the form of electrodynamics, chemistry or planetary motion. If God's experiences were representative then the rules of the immigration cycle might apply to politics, economics and the world of anthropology too. The prospect was enticing. In fact the *Universal Theory* would be a perfect candidate for the secret project he had presented to the angels when God first set off on His journey of discovery.

After all the complaints, God was delighted to see that things were improving. It might be the last time He was able to influence Gabriel's thoughts and if His successor could find a way of dealing with immigration he could solve more than the difficulties encountered by one individual during His time in London. The Arab-Israeli conflict, the internal squabbles in Northern Ireland and global warming would disappear, cold fusion would be rendered redundant at a stroke. Equally important, if Heaven were kept busy then God would be free to pursue His private affairs as He wished.

"What are You going to tell her?" Gabriel asked, breaking into his Master's thoughts. Not that it made any difference but he was curious. The taxi driver would never believe His fantastical stories.

So they did know, God smiled to Himself. His deepest meditations must have found their way into public thoughts. Well, it wasn't surprising, how could He expect to keep such a big thing secret?

"I don't know," He said and made ready to leave.

*

Red sky at night. Gabriel offered a sign to send Godwin Godfrey on his way. The clouds had cleared and a spectacular sunset illuminated the fields as London's latest immigrant followed the path slowly down Primrose hill. He would be on his own from this moment forward but it was a nice gesture.

It felt like a long way as Godfrey trudged across the park towards his flat, shivering in the aftermath of the storm. It was foolish to be outdoors but he had made his choices and taken control. Everything that happened from now on would be his responsibility. Everything would be his fault.

Back at home, he found pyjamas and huddled beneath the sheets. On this evening, there would be no time for reading. He looked into the abyss, one small step...

He was asleep by the time his head hit the pillow. Dreams raced around trying to find an accommodation with the new reality. His sleep became restless as his mind struggled to deal with problems, battling demons and fighting unlikely battles. Thoughts and ideals shuffled around. Could his earthly existence be an illusion? Had Gabriel told anyone? Would Michael play his part? Some questions were easier to resolve than others. He needed to know how much of his new life was down to his own efforts. It could be that Gabriel had sent him the job, the flat, or arranged the chance meeting with his taxi driver.

Midnight passed and Godfrey slept on, peaceful and warmer with every passing minute.

CHAPTER THIRTY SEVEN

GODFREY WOKE AS USUAL BEFORE THE ALARM CLOCK AND pressed ahead with his routine. He had things to do and there was little time to think about the night's activities. Dreams, he had found, could be difficult to remember and not quite so important in the morning. It didn't matter whether Gabriel was anxious or if Michael's temper had burnt itself out. He had a job to get to and couldn't waste precious energy worrying.

The Today programme was in progress and he was ready when *Thought for the Day* arrived. The pips finished, his signal for departure. There was no need to bother with the headlines; it would be easy enough to catch up once he got to work. He checked he had money, locked the door and set off for the office in good time. Mostly, he was thinking about his luck on the previous day. If he hadn't been late and if it hadn't been raining. If if if… but he couldn't deny that he was pleased with the way things had worked out. Now that he had dealt with Gabriel and Michael, the issue of clothes for the weekend wouldn't be a problem.

The lights were neither for nor against him and it was cloudless as he strode smartly along making good time on the first day of the rest of his life. He felt like one of those posters – *Life is a journey, not a destination* – a cliché but undoubtedly true. As he walked, he couldn't help wondering whether the attainment of his first ideal would send him back into another *no* phase. As yet, there was no indication. He bought coffee and treated himself to a pastry, something he wouldn't be doing every day. He had good reason for wanting to keep in shape.

By the time he reached Fleet Street his thoughts had moved on to the weather prospects for the weekend. Not that he was worried. Godfrey knew from long experience that good is simply what one hopes for and that rain or sunshine could be equally enjoyable. All in all, his mood was buoyant when he reached his desk without having encountered significant opposition. He was still smiling as he sat down a few minutes early, optimism had given him wings.

"Two days in a row, God, that's a record."

"Hello, Rebecca, how are you?" he said.

"Fine, fine. Up late last night and in again early today. Only a few hours sleep, unfortunately."

"Oh dear, more calamities?" God should have

noticed how tired they all were. He had been wrapped up in his own problems while life continued inexorably on. "What's been happening in the world?"

"You didn't hear?" she couldn't hide her amazement.

"I was out yesterday and I wasn't concentrating on the news this morning."

"Oh, I see, something to do with this big smile you've been wearing recently?" Rebecca had a facility for happiness. Even when she was exhausted, she still managed to remember what was most important.

"In a way, yes," Godfrey blushed.

"I understand. Say nothing but I'll be discreet if you want to tell me." She was laughing.

"I see. Like yesterday?" he couldn't help responding to her enthusiasm. "I suppose I should ask how you managed to change my email address?"

She touched a finger to her lips.

"Actually, I wanted to say…" he hesitated. "I know it seems silly but do you mind calling me Godfrey? The other name reminds me of the past and I'd like to move on. Do you know what I mean?"

"I'm so sorry," it was her turn to be embarrassed. "I was trying to help and now I've put my foot in it."

"No, don't worry, I enjoyed the joke. It's only that I was thinking last night. I would prefer to be Godfrey, that's all," he said. There was no point going into details. "So what happened, what kept you at work so late?"

"Earthquakes, volcanoes and generally the worst weather on record. Some kind of cosmic shift. No, that can't be right. They should have said 'seismic shift'. But I believe there was a cosmic storm too. Don't you love it when everything goes wrong and the experts are confounded? Makes for great interviews."

"Humph," was all Godfrey had to offer.

They both went back to work, she to the collation of weather information and he to the task of clearing his inbox. There was still no sign of a phase of rejection and he was feeling good despite upheaval in the rest of the world.

"Rebecca, you know this business with the weather?"

"Yes?"

"Well, I walked in this morning and it was fine."

"Oh, it's okay now," she looked over. "The strange thing is that it happened really fast and we're back to seasonal averages everywhere, except... no, everywhere basically. Apparently it's a self-correcting blip and the scientists are adjusting their models so they won't look silly next time. They sound like little boys playing with a train set, don't you think?"

"Thanks." There was more he would have liked to have said.

"For?"

"You know, for telling me, for being a friend. That sort of thing."

"I'll try to be more careful in the future," she was trying to be serious. "Are you sure there are no secrets you need me to keep?"

"Don't worry. I'll hang on to the few I have left," he couldn't help but feel pleased.

The office settled into its routine, taking Godfrey along. The day passed quietly and pleasantly and he arrived home a few hours later, looking forward to a peaceful night. For the first time he slept without the weight of responsibility hanging over his head. He dreamt only of coffee with Rebecca and advice about his clothes.

It was Thursday morning when Godfrey woke, feeling rested and looking happier than ever before. He hadn't made any demands on his new life and was enjoying every unpressurised moment. The test would come when his expectations escalated on the weekend.

"Godwin, would you mind?"

The director of the agency was at Godfrey's desk.

You could tell he wasn't used to mixing with low-level staff – nobody used the name Godwin. Rebecca looked up. All around the room, journalists and copywriters were taking note of the unusual activity and wondering if a Save-the-Sage campaign was going to be needed. Godfrey didn't do much most days but he was better than any search engine when something unusual came up.

The pressures of running a business could force administrators into decisions they couldn't justify even to themselves. Godfrey, however, had no experience of running a commercial enterprise and he was unaware of any intrigue that might surround him. Besides, he had always got on well with management. It was the director's lunch and advice about the Dead Sea Scrolls that had won him his escape ticket from the world of sandwiches. With a vague sense of anticipation, he made his way from the open-plan research station to the corner office for his chat with the man who had made it happen.

"Sit down, Godwin, sit down," Jim, the director, was a balding executive devoted to triathlons and his twin girls. He was on his feet, looking pensively at the view over the Thames while his co-worker sat waiting. "The weather has finally settled down. The storm last night caused havoc with our systems but that's not what I wanted to talk to you about. You don't mind being called Godwin, do you?"

"I answer to any name really, but most people call me Godfrey."

"Curious. Why do they do that? A little old-fashioned, I would have thought." Only last week there had been advice from Human Resources about the use of inclusive behaviour in the workplace.

"I don't mind. I'm much older and Godwin doesn't sound real. I suppose it must be something like that."

"I see," the director was still distracted. 'I'll call you Godfrey too, then, shall I?"

"That's fine. Whatever you like."

"How old are you anyway? You look about my age," Jim wondered out loud.

It didn't matter to Godfrey. His boss was somewhere in his early fifties, that could be about right.

"Ha ha, to those twenty-somethings we're ancient history. Very funny. They'll get here soon enough."

Godfrey could tell he wasn't required to participate. The director was a busy man and needed time to gather his thoughts.

"I'm presuming you don't have much on the go," Jim said, still thinking about the HR memo. He brought his mind back to the matter at hand putting to one side the suspicion he had overstepped the mark with discussions about an employee's personal circumstances.

"Nothing at all. Unless you count clearing my inbox every hour."

"Good, good."

Belatedly Godfrey remembered the advice not to undersell himself. Rebecca and Andy from the sports desk had warned him after the last big round of redundancies. Still, he was feeling optimistic and couldn't bring himself to worry although he needed the job now more than ever.

"This is all a little awkward," Jim cleared his throat, something about Godfrey made him feel like a schoolboy acting up. "What I'm saying is… I think I need your help. I have a proposition. It's different to our normal projects, so tell me what you think."

"No problem," Godfrey tried to help the conversation forward, "I promise to be honest."

"Oh good, yes, thank you. That will make it easier." The director did his best to smile. "A leader for one of our bigger accounts. Usually, they're a straightforward news feed but this time they've asked for something special. I gave my promise but all of a sudden we have operating issues. The fact is, I don't have anyone to turn to and it's not simple availability. It's a tricky brief and I'm not sure our regular reporters are right for the project."

Alarm bells were jangling in Godfrey's head. Already? It sounded like Gabriel was trying to help by sending work his way and he certainly didn't want that. He wanted to make it on his own. The alternative, he realised, was that Heaven had got itself into trouble. But that was unrealistic, it was too early for things to have gone wrong. In any case, there was no way he was going back.

"I know you don't have formal experience but I'm under pressure here and I would count it as a favour if you would help," the director finished his pitch. He might be the manager but he found himself waiting anxiously.

"Hold on," Godfrey was saying, "I need to think." He didn't want to sound ungrateful. It could be a great opportunity but he had to know what was going on.

"Do you want to hear the particulars. Shall I explain what it's about?"

"I suppose so. Really, I need to know about the client. There are some organisations I can't work for."

"A journalist with scruples? That's new." This time Jim managed a proper laugh. "G-20. Murphy, ex-

State Department, usually looks after the account but he's been trapped by this freakish weather. Had to be airlifted out of Etna when the storm broke, or so I'm told. Apparently it wasn't due for eruption and he was caught unawares. It's a volcano, for pity's sake. What was he doing inside?"

All a little vague, Godfrey thought sceptically. Gabriel and Michael could have arranged any background they wanted. He tried to keep an open mind.

"I need to know when you received the request." If the call had arrived recently, it would be more than a coincidence.

Jim, manager, director, turned to look at his reluctant employee. Negotiations were taking longer than he had anticipated. "All right then, I suppose you have a right to know. He's been sitting on the story for a month and now the fat is in the fire. When I get hold of him, he'll wish he stayed on that bloody mountain."

"One month?"

"Unbelievable, isn't it? Now he has disappeared and I'm left scrambling for an outline by the end of the week. I realise it's short notice."

"I think you should tell me everything," Godfrey put aside his concerns. It sounded like a job he could enjoy.

The director was relieved. You could never tell with workers these days but Godfrey had always been dependable. Should have asked him in the first place.

"Great, thank you. And, don't worry, I'll sort out your compensation."

"Compensation?" it was Godfrey's turn to look confused. Nobody had ever introduced him to the administrative term for salary, payment, whatever it took to keep staff focused through a long working day.

"Aren't you interested? Don't you want to know how much we'll offer if you take a full-time position?"

"Naturally," Godfrey had to say. He reminded himself to behave normally but he had never really been interested in money.

The interview ended and Godfrey wandered back to his desk with the details of his task. It was a familiar topic and he wouldn't need much research. Still, it would be tricky to get done so quickly. He needed to get started.

When he glanced around, there were concerned faces everywhere. One or two were edging closer to see if they should offer commiserations.

"Everything okay?" Rebecca asked. She was closest.

"Quite exciting, actually. I've got something new to work on," Godfrey said happily.

"Then you're staying? We thought you were being told to go. We were preparing to storm the ramparts."

"Not at all. In fact, it sounded more like a promotion," he stood to wave to well-wishers around the room. "You tell them, Rebecca, you know it will take ages if I have to send a message."

Godfrey couldn't help but admire the speed with which she disseminated information. The entire office breathed a sigh of relief. His absence from the union list was overlooked, that could only be a temporary oversight and would be corrected in due course.

Godwin Godfrey's new life would brook no interruptions and he drew up his seat to start the new project. Poverty, Probity and Profit. Jim had asked for broad brush stokes and a framework with a modern slant but it would be a pity to leave out historical detail that could illustrate the progress of moral purpose. The big question was how far back to go – where and when to start? He pushed the keyboard to one side and picked up a pencil. It would have to be longhand.

"In the Beginning…" he wrote.

EPILOGUE

GODFREY PUT ASIDE HIS WORK AND LAY BACK TO WATCH the dappled light playing across the room. His mind was drawn back over his career and experiences since that first day in the sunlight on Primrose Hill.

Next to him, Madeleine's breathing was deep and peaceful as she enjoyed the afternoon sleep that had become a feature of their weekends. She looked rested and her perfume was the scent of happiness. He knew how much he owed to luck but any success he'd managed to achieve could all be traced to her.

He slid down underneath the covers, getting as close as he could and trying not to wake her. He thought of loneliness and solitude, and a misplaced desire for greatness. Who could compare life to some vainglorious ambition? To love is to be, to be is to love. His mind flitted and danced with the motes in the sunlight, thinking of what had been and what might be still. He had no fear of ideals; he was no longer an immigrant and the dangers of dreaming wildly were slight.

She stirred at his side. Perhaps he had woken her

with his incurable habit of thinking out loud.

"Hmmm." She moved closer, pulling his arm over her so that they were one.

He lay still, knowing how precious an afternoon rest could be.

"Are you still working?" she murmured sleepily.

"I'm here, with you." And he was, in every way.

"It doesn't matter what they think, Godfrey. You can do it, I believe in you."

THE UNIVERSAL THEORY OF IMMIGRATION

No phase in which the immigrant tries unsuccessfully to achieve goals imported from his or her past.

Reasonable Options phase in which the immigrant asks questions that avoid the possibility of rejection.

Contempt for the New Society phase in which the immigrant feels more comfortable having made progress under *Reasonable Options* but is still not committed to the new society.

Resurrection of the Old Ideals phase in which *Contempt for the New Society* leads to a resurgence of unrealistic ambitions. The immigrant returns to the start of the cycle.

*All
the events
described in this book
actually happened. Only names
have been changed. But
then, what's in a
name?*
AB

l
o
n
d
o
n

January 2016

Acknowledgements

With grateful thanks to:

Ron Callow and Simon Buchanan at Design23
Sally Orson-Jones
John Bailey
Rebecca Souster and the team at Clays
Heather O'Connell
Rupert Harbour
Ben Cameron
Daunt Books in Marylebone

ADAM BETHLEHEM
Once a doctor, a student of physics, still an enthusiast for
irrelevant connections. Lives in central London.
The family motto: wake early; dream of fire; and, some day,
have a dog.

Also available:

Ben seeks refuge from intrusive memories in the world of his imagination. Life changes when he meets Holly at a party in London – the invasion of his thoughts is complete when she appears beside him in a favourite dream. He introduces her to Albert Einstein who seems to approve of his ambitions.

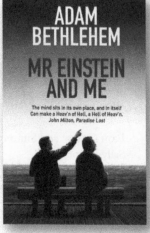

The silver lining of new-found happiness is threatened by the great cloud of times past. But assistance is at hand. From Mr Freud's famous couch, Ben must overcome the prejudice of privilege if he is to reclaim Holly…

> *"Screw Freud. He's got no right to invade, taking charge with his cigars and superior manner. So what if I like Holly? There has to be a motivation and, all of a sudden, sex isn't enough for him."*

Review by Julia Harrison – Bookseller at Daunt Books

"Set in the 1980s during the apartheid era, *Mr Einstein and Me* follows the fortunes of Ben, who has left South Africa to pursue his medical training in London … Adam Bethlehem throws a lot of his own experience, and passions into this novel. In setting the scene so well, he draws the reader into Ben's world. So much so in fact, that I raced through the surreal, and funny dream sequences, in which Ben seeks advice from Einstein, et al, in order to get back to finding out how things are going with his new love, Holly."

Publishing 2017:

Joshua Jones is a successful man whose mission is to answer the great questions of life, his singular failing being an inability to produce the son who will be his heir. Undeterred by the birth of a succession of daughters, he pursues his ambition with characteristic determination believing that nothing can be so uplifting as the triumph over a difficulty.

Whereas Jones is invigorated by the struggle, his wife (Martha) is worn out by their robust efforts at procreation. The introduction of pleasure into the realm of reproductive mechanics demonstrates that frivolity has a place in the world, a discovery that disrupts the certainty of the family's otherwise ordered existence.

Jones resolves to overcome the demons that threaten his position believing that reason will enable him to triumph. However, his achievements in the wider world carry little weight at home and the seeds of his downfall are contained in the very educative philosophy with which he attempts to lead his family from the abyss of an ordinary life

DESIGN 23

CREATIVE FOR PUBLISHING

Design 23 has 30+ years experience
producing design in publishing
for books, literature and screen.
Let us help turn your work into
the finished product.

5th Floor
230 City Road
London EC1V 2TT

07525 400244

info@d23.co.uk

Clays *Making Books Beautiful for 200 Years*

editorial | design | print | distribution | publishing consultancy

Being a successful independent publisher is all
about developing publishing skills and surrounding
yourself with people who can help you to make
your book the best that it can be.

That's where we fit in.

Clays is a market leading book production
specialist with an arm dedicated to working
closely with independent publishers.

Get in touch to find out how we can help you.

www.clays.co.uk | 02079026474 | @ClaysSelf_pub

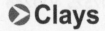